Also by Susan Price

The Sterkarm Handshake
Elfgift
Elfking
Foiling the Dragon
The Ghost Wife
The Bearwood Witch

Visit Susan Price's website at
www.susanprice.org.uk

Scholastic Children's Books,
Commonwealth House, 1-19 New Oxford Street,
London, WC1A 1NU, UK
a division of Scholastic Ltd
London ~ New York ~ Toronto ~ Sydney ~ Auckland
Mexico City ~ New Delhi ~ Hong Kong

First published in the UK by Scholastic Ltd, 2002
This edition published by Scholastic Ltd, 2003

ISBN 0 439 98246 4

Typeset by Falcon Oast Graphic Art Ltd, East Hoathly, East Sussex
Printed and bound in Great Britain by Cox and Wyman Ltd, Reading, Berks.

10 9 8 7 6 5 4 3 2 1

CONTENTS

1

THE BATTLEFIELD

Above, the sky glowed with the last fierce, sinking light of the sun. Below, Brother Dominic could not see where he put his feet. He trod on outspread hands, stumbled on legs.

He kept his lantern hidden within a fold of his cloak, fearing its light might be seen by the others who wandered the field. The ravens had left with the daylight, flying back to their roosts full of carrion – but with the darkness had come wolves, drawn by the scent of meat, eager to eat, their eyes glinting red when they caught the light. There were human wolves too – looters who went among the bodies, stripping them of clothes and armour, cutting off fingers to steal rings. If they found any alive, they murdered them.

Now and again Brother Dominic uncovered the lantern and cast its light at his feet. All too often it lit horrors: a face slashed and hacked, a body butchered. "Lord of Peace," Brother Dominic prayed, "give me courage for this work." He did not want to be there, in the dark, among the dead. But, hearing the cries of the wounded – cries of pain, cries of terror – he had asked himself: *Who will help them if I do not?*

He had gathered a party of monks and led them on to the battlefield, where, for an age, as the light faded, they struggled to find those that cried. Stumbling, throwing out a hand to catch himself, Brother Dominic had touched cold, slippery flesh and wet, thick blood. Coming on heaps of bodies, the monks had set down their lanterns and heaved aside the corpses, to find the living man who cried among them. They sweated at their work, and they were smeared with mud, with blood, with brains, but they worked on. Two by two Brother Dominic sent his monks back to the camp, carrying the wounded with them. Now he was alone.

He felt his loneliness sharply. At a distance a faint light bobbed, but on this side of the field it seemed he was the only living man. A chill breeze passed him, and he could not help but think it filled with ghosts. "God keep my soul," he said, crossing himself, and his voice broke on a sob.

His face was wet with tears. He had been

crying quietly for hours now, the water pouring down his face. It was hard to see so much death and pain in one place. So many piled corpses, and all of boys and young men who had hardly lived before feeding ravens and wolves. He wept so freely that he did not think he would be able to stop. No matter to what side he turned, there was more hacked flesh and splintered bones, more dead.

A voice called, "To me! Help!"

Though the voice was not loud, it sounded strong. Gladly, Brother Dominic turned towards the sound. To be able to take one more man back to the living would be a great joy.

He caught his shin on a discarded shield and clambered over a wall of silent bodies – and then the voice called out again, almost at his feet. "Here!"

The monk uncovered his lantern and shone its light down. There he saw a white face and two blue eyes looking up at him. They blinked in the sudden light. A spread of red hair surrounded the face, soiled with blood and dirt. A red beard hid the chin.

But then the lantern, swinging from Brother Dominic's hand, shifted its light. The monk expected to see the glint of a chain-mail coat,

3

or the dull buff of a leather jacket sewn with iron rings. But there was nothing below the head.

A body lay beside it, wearing a chain-mail coat sewn with gold links. A shield was still on the body's arm, but its head had been hacked off. So the head's eyes were open in death, not life. The blinking of its eyes was nothing more than a trick of the shifting lantern-light. The monk drew his cloak about his light once more, and would have moved on.

"Help me!"

The voice came from his feet. Brother Dominic shone his lantern down again and saw the severed head. Its eyes blinked. Its lips moved. "Help me, I beg you!"

The monk felt that he had been doused in a bucket of cold, cold water. His heart lurched with shock. His breath stopped in his throat. On his head, the hair moved, each hair rooted in a particle of ice. "Oh, Father, Son and Holy Ghost, protect me!"

The head spoke again, its lips moving impossibly. "Leave your prayers!" it said. "I mean you no harm – I will do you none. I can do you none! But I must have your help."

Brother Dominic reminded himself that his

God was always with him, and took courage. Bending over the head, feeling that he was in a dream, he said, "What is it you want from me?"

"Give me the news. Is my king alive?"

More than one king had fought in the battle that day. "Name your king and I will tell you, if I know."

"King Penda Wartooth!" said the head.

Brother Dominic crouched down. "He is alive, but badly wounded, I hear. And he is captive. King Edgar won this fight."

"Then I beg you," said the head, "take me to my king, take me to Penda!"

"That will be hard to do." The monk waved his hand before the staring eyes. "Can you see me?"

"I see you well enough," said the head, "in your Christian clothes, with your cross about your neck. I know you for a Christ-man – King Edgar's man!"

Brother Dominic nodded. "Do you know what has happened to you? Do you know that –?"

"That I have been pollarded – my head lopped? I know!" said the head. "I know."

"And yet you look at me with eyes that see. You talk. How can this be?"

"I have a promise to keep," said the head. "Until I have kept it there can be no rest for me, whether my head be on my neck or no!"

"There must be magic in this," said Brother Dominic. "And it is no Christian magic."

"Don't Christians teach that the dead will rise?" the head demanded.

"Not in bits and pieces. How can I take you to my camp? How do I know what danger or ill luck will come of my taking you there?"

"You don't know me," said the head. "So why should you trust me? But I think you will know *of* me when I tell you my name. I am Egil Grimmssen."

"What? The poet? King Penda's storyteller? Not that Egil Grimmssen?"

"I am – I was – that Egil Grimmssen," said the head. "And if you know that much of me, then you know that – even though I am not a Christian and I have no Latin – I am a man of learning."

"You have that reputation," said the monk. "Or had."

"You'll know that I am a man of my word, and always was. I swear to you by all my Gods, by my father's head and my mother's heart, I swear to you that if you carry me to my king,

I will do you no harm – nor any harm to your king or any of his people. I swear this to you."

"I don't think I would be allowed to take you to your king, but – since you are Egil Grimmssen, and since you give me your word – I will take you to my king. Indeed, such a miracle as you are, I think I *must* take you to my king."

"That will be enough," said the head. "This tongue in my head has never failed to win the favour of kings. Take me to your king and let me plead my case with him."

Brother Dominic straightened and looked about him. The light had gone from the sky and it was full dark. Not a sound came from around him, not one moan, not one cry. It seemed there was no one else to be saved.

"Very well," he said. "I will carry you to my king." Stooping, he lifted the head up gently, his hands cupped about its skull. He settled it in the crook of his arm and wrapped his cloak about it. He had become too dirty while wandering the battlefield to worry about a little more blood staining his clothes.

Shining the lantern at his feet, and taking care where he trod, he made his way back to King Edgar's camp.

2

THE HEAD TELLS OF
ITS FORMER LIFE

The head lay on a table, on a cushion of its own hair, which gleamed red and gold in the candlelight. Its open blue eyes shone glassily, and, as it blinked, its lashes were fine gold wires.

At the blink, King Edgar started back – but then stooped closer to the head, peering. "It cannot be."

Brother Dominic said nothing, but stood with his hands folded in his sleeves.

"You say it spoke?" the king asked.

"I spoke," said the head.

The king jumped back.

"I am Egil Grimmssen," said the head. "The sworn man of King Penda Wartooth. You won the battle, King, and I ask you for one small favour – given with the generosity of a victor! I ask not for gold or horses or ships – which so rich a king as you could easily give, but which I could no longer use. No! I wish to test your worth harder than that!"

King Edgar sighed. "What is it you ask?"

"Only that you take me to my king, to Penda."

King Edgar came close to the table and sat beside it on his stool. "Why should I give you to my enemy?"

"Why should you not? What am I worth? Carrion, fit only to be thrown on a dung-heap or buried in a hole. You will lose nothing by giving me away, and Penda will gain nothing."

"Penda will gain the advice of the dead," said King Edgar. "How can I tell what wisdom you may whisper in his ear?"

"I will whisper to Penda nothing but a story," said the head. "Last night, before the battle – Gods! Was it only last night? It seems a hundred years ago. But, last night, when we knew we were to fight in battle, he asked me for a story, to pass away the time of waiting. I gave him – it hurts to remember it now – I gave him a short answer. My mood was not for telling stories or singing songs. A foreboding lay on me, a heavy weight between my shoulder blades, a darkness hanging above my head. Never have I looked forward to battle less!"

"You foresaw your own fate," said King Edgar.

"Oh no, King! I thought it was Penda's death that crept up my back on little cold feet – I thought it was defeat that froze me. 'Don't pester me for stories now,' I said. 'I want to sleep.' 'That was not the answer I looked for,' said my king, and I told him, 'Tomorrow night, after the battle, I will tell you any story you wish to hear, and as many as you like. I swear it, I give you my word'. And then I wrapped myself in my blanket and lay down and pretended to sleep – indeed I slept not for a moment! Nor can I sleep now. I must keep my promise. Take me to Penda."

"Answer me a question," said King Edgar. "Why such devotion to this king of yours?"

"I am – I was – his sworn man," said the head.

"I have many sworn men. But I think all of them would hold that death ended their vows to me. I don't think that one of them would open their eyes or speak one word once their head and neck had parted company, only to keep a promise to me. And such a slight promise! A story!"

"King Edgar, if a shipwright wished to make you a great gift, he would make you a ship. A goldsmith would make you a brooch of gold. An armourer would make you a sword. My gift, King, is for learning and telling stories – and so I wish to tell my king the story he wished to hear. Penda once gave me a great gift. In return I owe him my deepest loyalty."

"I give my men many gifts," said King Edgar. "A king must be generous to keep his men. I hand out gold rings, and shields, and horses—"

"Piffling gifts," said the head. "Chickenshit beside what Penda gave to me."

"Oh? And what did Penda give to you?"

"Why," said the head, "Heartsease."

King Edgar looked up at Brother Dominic.

"There is a little herb," said the monk, "with a pretty flower, used to physic weak hearts. That is called Heartsease."

"Will you hear the story?" asked the head. "The story of how King Penda granted me Heartsease?"

King Edgar stood again, wary. "Are you trying to lay a spell on me?"

"Only this spell," said the head. "That if the story entertains you, you will give me to my king, so I can keep my promise."

"We are all under the Lord God's protection," said Brother Dominic, who was curious and wanted to hear the story. "Only the mercy of Our Lord God allows this miracle. I think we can listen safely."

King Edgar did not wish to appear more

cowardly than a monk. He seated himself on his stool again. "Tell your story."

"What will the storyteller's reward be? Will you take me to my king?"

"I promise nothing," said King Edgar. "A king must be more careful with promises than a storyteller. Let me hear your story first."

"Then cock an ear," said the head.

✳ ✳ ✳

"You'll have heard tell of me, King, that I'm an outlander. I was born in the Orkney Isles, and there my mother and father farmed, and fished, and had a good enough life. To make my story short, I'll tell you that my father died while I was too young to remember him, and my mother died when I was eleven. I'll say no more about that, though I could say much.

"My elder brother and I shared the farm and the work after that, and we got on as well as brothers ever do, until I took it into my head to be a storyteller and poet.

"Well, he laughed at me. In the Orkneys, every youngster fancies himself a storyteller and poet. The young men walk miles by moonlight and meet in wet, windy fields to swap rhymes and fancy phrases. They declaim epics to beached boats, and see themselves turning the girls' heads with words and being toasted at weddings and Autumn Feasts. My brother – his name is Eirik – couldn't believe I had it in me to be a poet. 'We're oxen, bred to pull the plough,' he said, 'not may-horses, decked for the feast. We've salt water in our veins and Orkney rocks in our heads, not poetry.'

"When I proved him wrong, he didn't like it.

"I first made my name among the young men of the islands. We would gather in the shelter of stone walls or in warm barns, or wherever we could get away from the older folk. We'd choose a subject and try who could make the best poem on it. They liked mine – and that was favour hard won. Every lad there wanted his own effort thought best and was slow to praise another's. It's been an easy life since I left Orkney. I tell you, kings are easier to please than those Orkney boys!

"Word spread, and when I was invited to a wedding or an Autumn Feast, folk challenged me to prove my reputation. And soon I was asked to gatherings. To weddings:

"To see her burning eyes,
Lift up the veil of linen –
Hurl the hammer
Into her lap!

"That's Thor's hammer, you Christ-men. Thor's hammer is put into the bride's lap at a wedding. And lifting the veil from the burning eyes – that's to make folk think of the story of how Thor dressed up as a bride – Oh, never mind. It got a big laugh at weddings in Orkney, but you wouldn't understand.

"I went to funerals as well:

"In the dark house
The table is spread with bread and beer.
The door stands open.
Enter, with no look back.

"At first I went to these feasts for nothing, pleased for a chance to speak my poems, have a drink and see the pretty girls. I wanted nothing more. But soon there were too many offers. I couldn't go to one, because I'd agreed to go to another. Or there was too much work at the farm, or I didn't feel like travelling so far. And then people started to say, 'Come to us and we'll give you a flitch of bacon,' – or a bundle of dried fish, or enough grain to fill your kitchen chest with flour.

"Ah, that's a dizziness, King, to know that folk will pay in fish or grain to hear your words! You kings, you hand out gold that you haven't mined or worked for – it means little to you. But my Orkney people, they'd gone out and caught those fish, and hung them up to dry. They'd grown that grain, and every measure they gave to me would be a measure that wouldn't be there to feed them through the winter. They truly wanted to hear my words.

"Even my brother saw the value of my poems, once folk were willing to pay. Then he agreed that I should go to the feasts, even if it meant taking ship to outlying isles and being away for weeks.

"And when the Lord of the Isles himself asked me to his hall for New Year and kept me there a week! Then I knew I had won fame. I told stories every evening for the lord and his guests, and made new poems for them every day, and the lord gave me two big gold armlets and a gold chain. After that the people couldn't get enough of me. There was hardly a wedding, or a Naming Day, or a funeral or a feast that I didn't attend. People would pay me to come and speak my old poems, and they'd pay me even more to make a new one especially for them. I was travelling all the time and filling my belly with the best. I'd come home, riding the horse someone had given me, and there would be Eirik, keeping company with our servants and slaves.

"They'd gather round and I'd tell them where I'd been, about how big the hall was where I'd stayed, about the coloured clothes of the guests and their gold and garnets and amber, about how much we'd eaten and drunk. The slaves' eyes would be as round as moons, and they'd forget to eat. I'd run through my poems and stories for them, and act the parts of all the people who came up to praise me and give me gifts – and the slaves would clap and cheer and say it was as good as being there.

"Eirik didn't enjoy it as much. 'You're away all the time,' he said. 'Everything's left to me. I can't be in two places at once – the slaves are getting slack because they know I can't check up on them all.'

"I gave him a gold ring, an amber cap-brooch and a small flask of wine, to make up for it. I thought he wouldn't be able to say anything after that, but he did. 'This is all very well while you're single, but what about when you marry? Children can't eat gold, a wife can't dress in wine. You'll have to work then.'

"Marrying was in my mind. There was a girl I had been courting, a farmer's daughter, named Oddi.

"Listen, King. Close your eyes and I'll make her stand before you. She's small, no higher than my shoulder, but with full, round, plump curves of a smooth pinkness, like a plump young piglet. Is anything smoother than a woman's back?

"Long, fair hair, with enough redness to make it shine like red gold. Her face – not the prettiest – and yet pretty – and white and pink – but what caught your heart was the impudence in it, the sidelong look, the flirting smile.

"I tramped over to her farm almost every night – through some terrible weather – but I would sooner be wet and cold than miss seeing her. We'd be bundled into bed together by her mother and father, and there we'd lie, cuddling and whispering and kissing – and the smell of old summers rising up from the straw mattress with every little movement! Remember those days, King? Weren't they better than anything that's come after?

"Anyway, Oddi's mother and father started hinting to me that it was time I either married Oddi, or let some other man have her. And I wanted to marry Oddi. I saw myself building us a house, either beside her parents' or over at our farm. . . I saw us raising a brood of youngsters, and me becoming a well-respected man and Oddi a fine matron with amber neck-laces that I'd earned for her – and by and by there would be grandchildren. It was not a bad life that I foresaw.

"But. . . But. . .

"Oh Gods, give me a long settled life like my father had – but not yet!

"I could have married. The Lord of the Isles himself hinted that, if I wished to marry, he would give me a little land . . . but the Orkneys seemed to me to be very small rocks in a very big sea.

"There were other lands. There were other lords. There were kings and kingdoms, who had never heard a word from me. And how they must long to! One night, when I was bundled in the wall-bed with Oddi, I asked her if she would wait for me if I went travelling overseas.

" 'I don't know,' she said. 'Why do you want to go?'

" 'To win fame!'

" 'But you're famous already, Egil.'

" 'Not as famous as I could be if I went to Denmark. Or England. The kings there would load me with gold. I would have to buy ships and pack-ponies to bring it back. And when I came back to Orkney – ! The people would line the roads to see me pass. I would be a bigger man than the Lord of the Isles himself!'

"She propped herself up on her elbow to look at me, with her long, shining hair falling down about her. I could see I had her interest.

" 'I would bring you back bales of silk in every colour. You could have a coloured dress for every day of the year. I'll bring you amber. Garnets.'

" 'Of course I'll wait for you,' she said, and kissed me. 'I love you. I wouldn't marry anyone but you.'

" 'You'll be the wife of the most famous poet in the world. I'll come back, and marry you, and take you to live in – in England. At the court of a king. You'd like that, wouldn't you?' "

She smiled – that cheeky, flirting smile, so I

saw that she would like it more than anything. We kissed on the agreement.

"The next day, I went to the Lord of the Isles and asked his permission to go. He wasn't pleased to lose me, he said, but his best wishes went with me. He proved it, too, by giving me gold for my travels and letters to English kings.

"My brother didn't give me his blessing. 'Oh aye, fly away to England and swan there,' he said. 'Leave me here alone, a sheep without shelter, battered by every wind.'

" 'I'll be back sooner than you think,' I said.

" 'Sooner than *you* think. "*Anything passes for wit at home*". They won't be so easily fooled overseas, you'll find out.' So we didn't part on the best of terms.

"It is hard to do a thing, but short to tell it. To shorten my story I shall say nothing of my seafaring, and my travels through dismal England. I shall say nothing of the lords and kings who listened to me and yawned. I shall jump over all that and take up my story again when I reached the court of King Penda Wartooth.

"Now King Penda is a man of great curiosity, and it was his habit, whenever a traveller came to his court, to talk to them about where they had come from, and where they were going, and what their business was. In this way he learned much about the world. So, when I arrived at his court, he made a point of calling me to his private rooms one evening, to ask me about myself.

"Folk might call this man a lord and this man a king, but men are all the same. They all pull down their breeks, squat over the hole and shit. Isn't that right, King? So I felt no unease. Many times I had talked with the Lord of the Orkney Isles, and any Orkney man is a king uncrowned. So I made myself at home in King Penda's rooms, and I told him of Orkney, and my travels, and the news and gossip of other courts.

"Many think the Orkneys a backwater, where nothing ever happens, but ships are putting in there from all over the north, bringing all the news, and I had been in the habit of talking it all over. 'You have an opinion on everything!' said King Penda. And he is a man who likes to talk, and argue, and discuss how things should be. 'Do you play chess?' he asked me.

"I did, so we played a game, and he beat me, I admit it. 'You won't beat me a second time,' I said. 'I have the measure of you now.'

" 'We'll see,' he said. 'Come along tomorrow night and we'll play again.'

"That's how our friendship started. Soon it was said – by whisperers in corners – that I was 'the King's favourite', with a sneer, as if I'd won his friendship by some sort of trick. The truth was, he is a good chess-player and I am a good chess-player, and we enjoyed playing against each other. And we enjoyed talking. I made him laugh. He was good company, and he found me good company. What trick is there in that?

"He enjoyed my poetry too, and my stories – he is something of a poet himself. Not in my class, but he shows promise. We'd talk over poetry, and swap rhymes and fancy phrases just like the lads back home in Orkney used to do. We'd be drinking ale, of course, and the more we drank, the higher the poetry flew! Those were grand nights. I never used any flattery or trickery to become King Penda's favourite. I was just me. Maybe that's what made some so jealous – that, despite their trickery and flattery, they couldn't take my place beside the king from me.

"I won't deny but I did well from the king's friendship. He dropped by the place I was lodging once, and said, 'You need a better place than this!' And lo! I was given a hall to myself in the Royal Residence, with benches, and a bed and hangings and everything. I lay on the bed and looked round and thought: this makes the old farmstead in Orkney look shabby!

"And once I had the hall, well, I needed something to keep it up. So the king made me an allowance. 'You're my poet now,' he said. 'Make me an epic or two. And get yourself some decent clothes.'

"When Eirik came over to visit me, I was living high on the hog. I'd sent word back to him of where I was, together with some gifts, but he never let me know he was coming. He arrived one day, at the Residence, and I was called down to the gatehouse, to say if I knew him or not, before they would let him in. There he was, in the gatehouse, wrapped in a thick travelling-cloak.

"'Who is looking after the farm now?' I said.

"'Oh,' he said. 'I left Old Daw in charge.' (That was the oldest of our slaves.) 'And Oddi's father's dropping by to keep an eye on things.'

"'Will the place still be there when you get back?' I said. 'Or will it have blown into the sea without one of us there to watch it?'

"'Somebody had to come and check up on you.'

"Well, I was more glad to see him than I had ever been in my life. I dragged him back to my hall, and when he saw the place, he looked as if I'd slapped him round the chops. 'The king must think we all eat, drink and shit poems,' he said.

I sat him down and poured him wine – 'Ale would have been good enough for me,' he said – and I asked him how Oddi was. She was well, was she? As beautiful as ever? Her little smile as cheeky as ever? Did she ever talk about me? 'Tell her that I think about her every day,' I said.

" 'She sent her best wishes,' said Eirik, 'and asked, when are you coming home?'

" 'Soon, tell her, soon. How long are you staying?'

" 'Oh, a few months,' he said.

" 'I'll show you a good time while you're here,' I said. 'I'll take you along to meet the king tonight.'

"That wasn't the best idea I've ever had. The king was polite and asked all about the farm, but Eirik answered in grunts. After an hour of it, the king looked at me from the corner of his eye with a sort of desperation, as if to say, *I can't keep this up for much longer.* I told Eirik that he must be tired and took him away to bed.

"I thought he'd grow more at home as time went on, but he didn't, not even when everyone knew him. 'Ah, you're Egil Grimmssen's brother,' people would say to him; and they'd turn to others and say, 'This is the storyteller's brother.'

"I thought he'd feel better if he looked more like the others at court, so I tried to lend him some of my better clothes and a brooch, a gold armband. 'All the jewels in the world won't make me any prettier,' he said, and 'Homespun suits a farmer better than silk,' – even though the tunic I'd offered him had been of fine wool, not silk.

"No more than a month had gone by before he told me he was leaving again, going back to Orkney. 'So soon?' I said.

" 'The sooner I get back, the sooner I can take your message to Oddi. When shall I tell her to look for you?'

" 'Oh, soon.'

" 'But when? Fix a time. The poor girl's pining.'

" 'Next year,' I said. 'Maybe.'

" 'Next year!'

" 'I can't throw up everything here and run back home! Tell her I'll come and fetch her. Tell her what I'll be bringing her to.' I waved my arms around my hall. 'This is a bit better than an Orkney farmhouse, isn't it?'

"He blew down his nose. 'Shall I tell her about Hildy?' Hildy was a slave-girl I had bought.

" 'No need,' I said. 'Hildy just looks after me.'

" 'I know she does,' he said. 'I've heard her.' On that, off he went. Nothing I could say would make him stay.

"The year went by, and I did think of going home, but the king had some ambassadors coming from Ireland, and he wanted me to stay around, and then I bought some land, and there were some legal things to attend to and, one way and another, it was eighteen months after I'd said goodbye to Eirik that I set off to Orkney myself.

"The closer I came to Orkney, the more I thought of Oddi. The more I thought of her face, and her body and her softness and her hair, and her giggle, and of cuddling up in bed with her, all warm and dark and smelling of homely straw. The nearer I came to Orkney's shores, it was as if I could smell her, as if I could feel her close warmth, and I grew mad for her. As soon as I was off the ship, I bought a horse and rode straight to Oddi's steading.

"Her father and mother made me welcome. 'Look who it is!' they said, and sent servants running to bring water to wash my face and hands, and food and drink. I was looking all around.

" 'How are you, lad?' cried her father, slapping me on the back.

" 'You look well,' said her mother, touching the fine linen of my tunic. 'You're dressed very handsome.'

" 'Where is she?' I asked.

"They were surprised. 'Where's who?' asked her father.

" 'Where's Oddi? Who else?'

"Now they looked at each other in shock and dismay. 'Hadn't you heard?' asked her mother. 'Didn't Eirik send you word?'

"Oh, the sickness I felt then. I had to reach out a hand and lean against the wall. It came to me that Oddi had died, that she was in her grave. I swear that the daylight pouring in through the open door turned dark to my eyes. 'What happened?' I said.

"They went on staring at me, her mother clutching her hands to her breast. 'Tell me,' I said.

" 'Eirik said he was going to send you word,' said her mother. 'She and Eirik were married last autumn.'

" 'Not long after Eirik came home from seeing you,' said Oddi's father.

"I had to sit down on a bench. 'Married? To my brother? Married?'

"Her mother sat beside me. 'They came to an agreement very quickly. They're happy. They have a little boy. They named him after you.'

"Gods! I had to get out of there. I don't think I was polite about my leaving.

"I mounted my horse and set off for my brother's steading – but I hadn't gone very far before I saw how shaming it would be to ride up there demanding to know what they'd been thinking about, to do this to me. So I turned the horse round and I was going to ride back to the shore and take ship again, and go back to England – but I hadn't gone very far that way before I thought of how the news was going to be reported. 'Egil came home, and left again, without even wishing his brother well of his wedding.' So I turned the puzzled horse again and started back along the way – but I couldn't face it. In the end I went to Oddi's parents and begged them to take me in for a few days. I think they guessed what the trouble was. They made me welcome and didn't ask many questions.

"After three days I had calmed down, and had mastered my feelings. I thought I could face my brother, and I rode over to the farm. Eirik himself came out of the house to greet me as I dismounted. 'Egil! We heard you were home! How much happiness it gives me to see you again!'

"I stood in front of him and looked him in the face. 'The first thing I must do is wish you well of your wedding,' I said. 'You didn't remember to give Oddi my message, then?'

"He looked confused. 'Message?'

"I had told myself I would be dignified, but I leaned into his face and said, 'When you ran home from England early because you couldn't stand to see your little brother doing well, I asked you to tell Oddi that I'd be home within a year, and to wait for me.'

" 'I don't remember that,' he said, and he didn't. You could tell from his face that he didn't remember it at all. 'You've been longer than a year,' he said. 'Come in and see Oddi.'

"So we went into the house. My first thought when I saw Oddi – if I'm honest – was that she was fatter than I remembered, and not as pretty. But then, as we talked, and as she laughed and looked sidelong at me through the smoke, and hugged her little boy with her chin resting on his head, I saw that she was just as I remembered after all. And I was so jealous, it was as if I had fighting cats in my belly. Everything I saw – Eirik leaning close to Oddi and smiling at her, the warm comfortable farmhouse, the little boy – everything I saw made me think: *this should have been mine*. And Eirik stole it from me. He ran home from England and went straight to Oddi and asked her to marry him. And she did!

"I told them about my life in England, how I talked with the king every night, of the gold and land I owned, of my plans for the future. . .

" 'That's nice,' Oddi said. 'You've done well for yourself.'

" 'I was doing it for you,' I said.

" 'For me?'

" 'All for you.'

" 'No,' she said. 'Don't tell yourself that tale. If you'd been thinking of me, you'd have come home and married me. I tired of single life, Egil. I tired of a cold bed. I have what I want, and I'm only sorry I waited as long as I did to get it. I don't envy you your talks with kings and your gold rings.'

" 'Then I shall have to give it all to some other woman,' I said.

"She raised her brows, smiled and said, 'Lucky her.'

"At that I got up and left. I went back to Oddi's parents, stayed with them another night and then rode down to the shore, where I took ship for England as soon as I could.

"But there was no settling back into my English life. I hated crowds, I hated their stupid laughter. I wanted to be by myself, quiet, in my hall. I did not go to talk with the king. When he sent for me, I sat silent, unable to think of anything to say. When he told me the news of all that had happened while I'd been away, I hardly bothered to listen. It didn't interest me.

" 'Egil,' he said, 'are you ill?'

"I told him that I was as well as I'd ever been.

" 'Then what has happened?' he asked.

"I didn't want to answer, I didn't want to talk about it at all, but he kept asking me and badgering me, until at last I had to tell him. 'I went home intending to marry, King. But the girl that I wanted had married someone else.'

" 'That's bad luck,' he said. 'I'm sorry I couldn't let you go earlier.'

" 'She married my brother,' I said. 'My brother married her. I told him to tell her I'd be home in a year to marry her, and he married her himself.'

" 'That's hard,' said the king, 'but perhaps he loved her.'

" 'He did it to spite me!' I said. 'And she – she said she would wait for me – and she married my brother!'

" 'I'm sorry,' he said. 'You must feel bad about it.'

"I did. My belly was full of fighting cats again. I couldn't sit still. I couldn't be civil. 'King,' I said, through gritted teeth, 'I'm sorry. I have to go.' And I went back to my hall and kicked stools about.

"Some days passed, and then the king sent for me again. 'Egil,' he said, 'I can't have you sulking about the court like this. What can I do to help you get over this? I could find you another bride.'

" 'No,' I said.

" 'Anyone, within reason, that you fancy. Look around. Choose a girl and I'll speak to her father for you.'

" 'No,' I said. 'If I can't have Oddi for my wife, I don't want a wife.'

" 'Well, what do you want instead? A title? There are heiresses I could marry you to, and make you a lord.'

" 'No,' I said.

" 'Land. Do you want land? I could marry you to an heiress with a good bit of land. It'd take your mind off things, looking after it. How about that?'

" 'I told you, I don't want a wife. And I don't want to look after land. I don't want to be a lord.'

" 'Then do you want to travel?' said the king. 'See new places, have adventures. That's probably the best thing. I'd be sorry to lose you again, but if you came back in a better frame of mind. . .'

" 'I don't want to travel.'

" 'I could fit you out a ship,' said the king. 'Fill it with trade goods. You could sail off and see strange places and make your own fortune! How would that suit you?'

" 'I can't be bothered with ships and trade goods,' I said. 'I just want to be somewhere quiet with no one bothering me!'

" 'How about a small farm?'

"'No!' I said.

"'You're not being helpful, Egil,' the king said. 'If none of these things will do for you, what do you want?'

"In a moment, then, I knew what I wanted. And it was a huge thing to ask. 'King,' I said, 'I don't want a wife, I don't want a title, I don't want land, I don't want a ship, or trade goods or gold or a farm – but I wonder if you will grant what I do want?'

"The king spread his hands. 'Ask.'

"'I want to talk,' I said. 'If I talk, will you listen?'

"'Willingly,' he said.

"'You haven't heard yet what I want to talk about. I want to come here, every night, and talk about Oddi and Eirik. Will you let me do that?'

"'Gladly,' he said. Kings aren't always wise.

"I started talking right away. I'd been so silent for weeks, but now words burst from me. I told him how I loved Oddi so much I would have done anything for her, how all the time I'd been here, at his court, Oddi had been in my mind. 'I worked for her, I bought land for her, I earned fame for her – but she betrayed me.' I warned him of the treachery of women. I told him of how much I had done for my brother Eirik, how I would have given him my last piece of silver, and how Eirik had betrayed me, and I warned him against the treachery of men. I told him that I saw nothing for me in the world now. I could trust neither men nor women. Maybe I should cut my throat or, if that was cowardly, maybe I should take his offer of a ship and go off round the world and try and find some sea-dragon or enemy who would put an end to me.

"The king listened to it all, and kept my cup filled with ale and, at the end of the evening, had a couple of men carry me to my hall and put me to bed.

"The next night I told the king that Oddi hadn't always been treacherous. I told him of how it had been when I had been at home, of the nights I spent bundled up in bed with her, of the nights sitting in the yard, talking. Of dancing with her at feasts. Of watching other men admire her. The light on her hair. How special her smile was – I spent an hour at least trying to describe her smile so he would understand how special it was. I told him of her little hands and plump little arms. I made poems about her breasts, about their warmth and thistle-down softness, the way they fitted my hands. I remembered things she'd said, clever things, and wise things and funny things that had made me laugh. I talked about her all night, and when the king tried to say something about a girl he had once loved, I said, 'Yes, but Oddi –' and went on talking about her. The king shook his head, shut up, and poured more wine. I wasn't as drunk that night. I was able to reach my hall by myself.

"The night after that I talked about Eirik. Maybe I'd been unfair about him, I said. He wasn't the worst man. After my parents had died he'd brought me up, and that couldn't have been easy for a young, single man. But then, could I help it if he was jealous of me? And it was that jealousy that had made him marry Oddi. He didn't love her! He was too old for her and had a mind no broader than his fields! What did she see in him? What had got into her that she'd agreed to marry him when she knew that I – or did she know? Had Eirik kept my return a secret so he could get in before me? A treacherous brother, taking advantage of a lovely girl! I hated him. I felt sometimes that I could kill him – and then Oddi would be a widow and could marry me. Would anybody blame me if I killed him? Didn't I have cause?

"I drank a lot again that night, and was once more carried to my bed. But the next night I went over to see the king again. I could see his face was strained, but I was so eager to talk that I didn't even ask him how he was. I'd been thinking that maybe I'd given him the wrong idea of Oddi – that she was a flirt, or hard-hearted. I started telling him about her all over again, how pretty she was and how taking were her ways. I wanted him to understand why I'd fallen for her in the first place, before I'd discovered what treachery was in her. I did notice that the king fidgeted a bit, tapped his fingers on the arm of his chair, but I didn't let it distract me.

"The next night I discussed Eirik with him, going over every bit of his character, how good he'd been to me as a boy, but how jealous of me after, and why, why had Oddi married him? The night after that, it was Oddi again. And the night after that, I asked him, did he think Oddi and I would ever be married? If Eirik died, say? Or maybe she would soon find out what he was really like and finish with him? Would she then think of me, maybe even send word to me? 'If she did, I'd go to her,' I said. 'It would mean putting aside pride, I know, but I would do it. If she sent word.'

"The king sighed.

"In short, for a month, I talked every night about Oddi and Eirik – oh, and about me.

"For another month I talked every other night.

"For a month after that, maybe once or twice a week.

"And after that, I found I didn't want to talk about it much at all. I'd talked myself out. Oddi had married Eirik and not me. She didn't want me. She wanted him. I knew it. I could face it. There came a night when I went along to see the king and said, 'Let's have a game of chess.'

" 'Don't you want to talk?' the king asked.

" 'No. I want to play chess.'

"I thought the king sighed again, but he caught it between his teeth, and reached for the chess board. He is a well-mannered man, King Penda.

"He won the game. When I rose to go that night, I said, 'King:

> 'You gave me no land,
> You gave me no rich wife.
> No ship you gave me,

38

Nor gold, nor silver.
You gave me Heartsease,
And my heart is yours.'

"Would you have had the fortitude of King Penda, Christian man? Could you have sat through all those long evenings, and spoken not one impatient word, not made one excuse? Could you have endured? Wouldn't it have been easier to have taken gold from your fingers and sent me away?

"That is why I am King Penda's man. That is why I must keep my promise to him. Take me to him, I beg of you. Keep your promise."

✠ ✠ ✠

"I made no promise," said King Edgar. "I must take counsel."

An expression of impatience passed over the head's face, but then it closed its eyes. "As it pleases you, King."

"Brother Dominic," said Edgar, "you see that shirt on the stool behind you? Wrap the head in that, if you please, and put it in that chest over there for safekeeping."

The monk did as he was asked and, as the

shirt wrapped the light from the head's eyes, it cried out, "Oh, let me keep my promise!" But once put into the chest, it made no more noise.

King Edgar sat silent in thought for a while, and then he said, "You will be returning to your monastery, Brother?"

The monk nodded his head.

"It will be a while before I return home," said the king. "I think the head will be safer in your keeping until then. Will you take it back to the monastery and keep it until I send for it?"

"Gladly, King," said the monk, with a bow.

"Then let that be the way of it," said the king. "Take it with you now."

And so the head of the storyteller passed into the keeping of the Christian monks.

3

THE HEAD TELLS A TALE
FOR THE MONKS

The monks were gathered, at evening, in their small dining-hall. The Father Abbot sat in the place of honour, at the high table, and before him stood Brother Dominic.

"This head, this severed head – am I to understand that it speaks?" said the abbot. "Without breath?"

"It is a miracle, Father."

"And the king has given it into our care?"

"It is in my bundle, outside the door," said Brother Dominic.

"Then fetch it here!"

Brother Dominic went to fetch his bundle. When he returned he found that the monks had been permitted to leave their seats and gather about the high table. They made way for Brother Dominic as he came to stand in front of the abbot.

He pushed aside dishes and laid the bundle on the table. Carefully, even reverently, he unwrapped it.

Some of the monks leaned around him to see better, even though some of them covered their eyes with their hands and peered through their fingers. Others stood back, having no wish to see what the bundle held.

As for the abbot, he leaned away and wrinkled his face in distaste, but once he saw the head, he sat up straight and his expression changed to one of sharp curiosity. "Not a pleasant sight," he said, "but it appears uncorrupted."

"It is a miracle," murmured Brother Dominic.

The head sighed, opened its eyes and looked at the abbot, who started. His hands, quavering in shock, thumped on the wooden arms of his chair. "Lord protect me!" he said, putting his hand to his heart. There were cries from the monks as they bobbed backwards in fright, and then bobbed forwards again, eager to see.

"May all your Gods protect you," said the head, its lips shaping the words. "But you need fear no harm from me."

Again the monks cried out. Some stepped back from the table, fell to their knees and prayed.

Glaring at Brother Dominic, the abbot demanded, "Is this some trick?"

"Why, no, Father Abbot! How could it be?"

"I have heard," said the abbot, "that some can throw their voices and make it appear that a cat or a cooking pot speaks. Are you playing that trick? Have you brought this piece of filthy carrion here so you can pretend that miracles happen in your presence?"

"My lord," said the head, "this piece of filthy carrion has never needed another to speak for it."

"Father Abbot," said Brother Dominic, "I don't know how to throw my voice! The king believed that the head could speak."

"The king is young," said the abbot, "and not well-read."

The head spoke up again. "Put it to the test. Send Brother Dominic away. Send away anyone you suspect of trickery or witch-work."

The abbot paused, considering. "Any trickster can pass a test he has himself devised. But we will try. Brother Dominic and any brother who followed the king on his campaign must leave the hall now. Go to the church and spend the time in prayer. And let someone fetch me here the Bible, and a flask of holy water from the font."

Brother Dominic, and those who had

accompanied him to war, filed out of the hall, and others ran away on the abbot's errands. While they waited, the abbot took the rosary of garnet beads from round his neck, and circled the head with it. The head sighed again, and closed its eyes. There was an outbreak of whispering among the monks gathered about the table. Had the Christian rosary silenced the magical head for ever?

A monk came in carrying the great leather Bible in both arms. Another followed behind him, holding a small leather flask of holy water.

The Bible was placed on the table and the head lifted up and set on top of it. The abbot pulled the stopper from the flask and spattered the head with holy water.

Its eyes opened again, and its face grimaced. "I am wet – cold and wet. A guest must be given water to wash – but must you soak him?"

"A trick, a trick," came the whisper from half the monks.

"A miracle, a miracle," whispered the other half.

"Do you need more proof, my lord?" asked the head. It turned its eyes from side to side, looking at the dishes on the table. "I see you have eaten. Now is the proper time for telling stories, after the evening meal. Shall I tell a story?"

"We listen only to the histories of Christian saints," said the abbot.

"And you think I know nothing of Christian saints, or will choke on the telling? Do you think I never had to entertain a Christian at King Penda's court? I am a king's storyteller. I know hundreds of stories, of every kind. Will you hear a story of a Christian saint?"

Coldly, the abbot nodded.

"Well," said the head, "with my friend, Brother Dominic, banished from me; draped in a rosary, perched on a Bible and drenched in holy water, I begin. . ."

✠ ✠ ✠

"You'll have heard of the Bright Wolf, the great King Kenulf of Mercia, who ruled well and wisely – don't all kings? – until he unluckily dropped down dead one day. Then his son, the Bright Helm, Kenelm, became king, although he was a child, a little boy of seven.

"But, my lord, he was a king, and so he ruled well and wisely. Every morning and evening he went to church, and he knew all the prayers, better than nursery rhymes. And after church, he didn't run off to play with his bat and ball, but went to the council chamber and spent all day listening to men argue about who had moved whose boundary marker, and who had stolen whose inheritance, and who owed who three days' work – I'm sure, my lord, you've heard the like.

"The little king was helped in his judgements by his foster-father, a man named Askbert, and by his older sister, a beautiful woman – well, she was a princess, so of course she was a beautiful woman – named Quendry.

"Now this man, Askbert, and this woman, Quendry, were lovers, and when they lay wrapped around each other in the dark of the bed-closet, certain things were whispered between them that could not be said in the hearing of others. Lovers' whispers – such as how a man should rule a great kingdom like Mercia, and not a little child, and what a shame that King Kenulf hadn't lived longer, to give dear little Kenelm time to grow. And how a splendid, rich kingdom like Mercia should have a beautiful queen, to graciously give gifts to the warriors who came seeking service.

What a shame that dear little Kenelm wasn't old enough to marry.

"How it would have been better for the kingdom of Mercia if Kenelm had died with his father – a dreadful shame, but better for the kingdom none the less. Then his sister, Quendry would have become Mercia's beautiful queen, and she would have married Askbert, and then Mercia would have had the king it deserved.

"Now it happened, soon after this, that little Kenelm had been put to bed by his nurse in his private rooms, when there was a knock at the door, and the sound of feet hurriedly moving away. The nurse, an old Welsh woman named Olwen, went to the door and opened it. No one was there, but on the floor of the passage stood a leather flask, which she picked up.

" 'Who was that, nurse?' asked the little king, from his bed.

" 'Whoever was there has run away,' she said, 'but they've left this.' And she showed him the flask, which was finely decorated with gold filigree-work. Pulling out the stopper, she sniffed. 'It seems someone has sent you a bed-time drink. I smell honey – and blackberries.'

" 'How do you know it's for me?' asked Kenelm.

" 'Who would leave it for me, in such a fancy flask?'

" 'Bring it here, then, and let me taste it,' said Kenelm.

" 'Oh, no, no,' said Olwen. She had spent her long life at a great royal court, and she was still alive. That meant she had learned a few things. She sat on the edge of Kenelm's bed and said, 'Call your dog here.'

"Kenelm's dog slept in a basket in a corner of the room. Kenelm called it, and it came, ears pricked and wagging its tail. Olwen poured a small pool of the honey drink from the flask on to the floor.

"The dog lapped it up, tail wagging ever more briskly, and seemed to enjoy it.

" 'Now we wait,' said Olwen.

"They waited for the time it might take a man to walk half a mile, and then the dog retched and writhed. Its writhings became convulsions. It vomited and choked; and it died.

"Kenelm cried for his dog, but Olwen said, 'Better the dog than you. It was no friend who left you that drink. Kenelm, you must be careful.'

" 'I am in God's Hands,' said little Kenelm. 'I commend myself to Him. He will take care of me.'

" 'From your lips to God's ear,' said Olwen, but, being a wise old woman, she knew that the Christian God – that all Gods – are modest and shy, and hang back, afraid to push Themselves forward and make a show. It's often quicker to help yourself. So Olwen went to see Kenelm's sister, the Lady Quendry, and his foster-father, Askbert, and told them about the poisoned drink, and watched them very close while she told her tale. 'Oh, dear God!' cried Quendry. 'My brother is in danger! We must find out who is trying to harm him! We must double the guard about him!'

" 'Tell no one else about this,' said Askbert. 'It may be easier to catch the traitor if he does not know we are alert.'

"Olwen promised to keep the story to herself, but she had her own suspicions, and was careful what she ate and drank after that. She touched nothing that did not come from the common dish at table. But no more fancy drinks or cakes or anything of that sort were left for Kenelm, and at table he had his food-tasters to protect him.

"Then, at the end of a day in the council-chamber, Askbert said, 'Let us not hold council tomorrow. Your sister has been worried that you are working too hard. She thinks that you and I should enjoy ourselves for a change, and go hunting. What do you think?'

"'Oh, yes, take me hunting!' said the little king. 'I should like that!'

"'Tomorrow then,' said Askbert. 'At first light. We'll have the whole day to ourselves, in the hills.'

"Kenelm ran to his rooms and told Olwen that he was to be up early the next day, because he was going hunting! 'That's a good idea, it'll put some colour in your cheeks,' she said. 'I'll be sure to wake you early, and I'll pack up a good dinner to take with you. And you'd better get a good night's sleep tonight.'

"But little Kenelm couldn't sleep, for excitement, and the snoring of old nursie beside him kept him awake. He had only just dropped off when Olwen was waking him again, saying, 'Come on now, time to get up if you're going hunting.'

"'Oh, Nurse,' he said, 'I had such a strange dream.'

"Now Olwen was a wise woman, as well as a

nurse, and she could often tell what dreams meant. 'What dream was that?' she said.

" 'Well,' said Kenelm, 'I dreamed I was out in the hills, hunting with Foster-Father Askbert. We were alone, we two. And I came on a tall, tall tree. It was all decked with flowers and shining lanterns, and was lovely to see. So I climbed it, to see the view from the top, and to be among the flowers and lanterns. Up and up I went, until I was in the topmost branches, and then I could see over all my kingdom – all the rivers and all the farms and hills and forests. A finer sight I never saw.

"'And then – a strange thing – one quarter of my kingdom rose up and bowed down to me. And then the second quarter rose up and bowed down to me. And the third quarter also. But the fourth quarter rose up and took a sharp hill edge into hands made of woods, and it chopped at the tree I was in, and chopped and chopped. The whole tree shook and I clung to the branches and cried aloud for help, but no one came. And then the tree was chopped through and began to fall – but I turned into a white bird and flew away. Nurse! Why are you crying?'

"For old Olwen was sitting up in bed with her hands over her face, crying and crying.

'Oh, little one,' she said, 'don't go hunting today. Stay here with me.'

"'But I want to go hunting.'

"'I can read what the dream means,' she said. 'The tall tree is the height and glory you will grow to if you live to be a man – oh, stay here with me, Kenelm! The three quarters of the kingdom that bow down before you are the people who love you – but the last quarter, that cuts down the tree, are the enemies who hate you and wish you dead. And the white bird is your soul flying away to another life elsewhere. Oh, stay here with me, Kenelm!'

"'But I shall be with Foster-Father Askbert!' said Kenelm. 'He will look after me. You are too fearful, Nurse. I put my faith in God. If He does not mean me to be killed, I shall not be. If He wants to call me to Him, then I must go.'

"And little Kenelm said his prayers, and ate his breakfast, and went off to hunt with his foster-father. Olwen begged and pleaded with him not to go, but he wouldn't stay.

"A large party, headed by Kenelm and his sister, Quendry, and their foster-father, Askbert, set off to hunt in the Clent Hills. All day they chased the deer over the hills, through the woods and fern, up on to the stony ridge and down into the valleys. And somehow it was that, during the chase, the party fell away, and Kenelm and Askbert were alone.

"They were riding through a wide meadow full of cows when Kenelm asked, 'Where has everyone gone? Where is Quendry?'

"'We've outdistanced them,' said Askbert. 'They can't keep up with us!'

"Soon it grew dark, and Kenelm said, 'I must say my evening prayers now.' And he dismounted, and knelt. Askbert dismounted too, but he didn't pray. He silently drew his sword, came up behind Kenelm and, as he prayed, chopped off the boy's head.

"He scraped out a grave beneath a nearby thorn-tree, dragged the body into it, kicked the head in beside it and covered them both.

"Then he rode back to the royal hall, shouting, 'I lost the king while we were hunting. Has he come home?'

"The Princess Quendry ran out, sobbing and pulling down her hair. 'Everyone thought he was with you! Oh, he is lost! My little brother is lost! We must search for him, we must find him!'

"Search parties were sent out, to ride about the hills and woods, searching for the little lost king. They didn't find him. They weren't looking under the thorn-bush.

"But the business of ruling a kingdom never stops, not even when the king is missing in the hills. Who was going to hold Council? Why, who else but Askbert? He was the king's foster-father. He would rule until Kenelm was found.

"Far across the sea, in far-off Rome, the King of all the Christians sat on his throne. I mean, the Pope. There he sat, in his palace, pontificating – and in through the window flew a white bird, a lovely white bird with a scroll in its beak. It dropped the scroll at the Pope's feet, and perched on his chair-back where it sang a most mournful song.

"The Pope picked up the scroll and opened it. He read:

> *Low in a mead of kine, under a thorn,*
> *Lies Kenelm, king-born,*
> *His head off-shorn.'*

"This poem had been written, I'm told, by powerful Christian spirits called angels. Forgive me, my Lord Abbot, but their powers don't lie in poetry, do they? Our pagan battle-sprites and earth-spirits are a rough lot, but they can turn a better rhyme than that."

"To make a good rhyme," said the abbot, "is not the greatest thing the human spirit can aspire to."

"I am rebuked," said the head. "And I go on with the story.

" 'This is a sign from God,' says the Pope. And he calls together some of his monks, and he orders them off to England, to find this mead of kine, and this thorn.

"The white bird went with them. When they travelled by land, it flew ahead of them, from tree to tree, glimmering; and when they went by sea, it perched in the rigging of the ship, shining. Once they were in England, it guided them, tree by tree, to Mercia, and it guided them through Mercia to a certain meadow where there were many cows.

"There they came on an old woman, who was herding cattle and, being hungry and thirsty, they asked her, Could they have a drink of milk from one of her cows?

" 'Oh, come with me, Masters,' she said. 'I have one red cow, who is such a good milker, you can have all you like.' And she led them away from the other cows, into a distant corner of the meadow and there, standing by a thorn-bush, was a red cow.

"The white bird perched in the thorn's branches, and sang its sweetest song.

"The old woman milked the red cow into her bucket, and the Pope's men stood astonished as such streams of milk gushed from the cow's teats that the bucket brimmed in a few blinks of the eye.

"'It's a strange thing, Masters,' said the old woman. 'For weeks now this cow has stood by this bush, and won't move a leg, and doesn't eat and doesn't drink – and yet she's in better fettle now than ever she was – and you see how much milk she gives!'

"The white bird still sang in the thorn's branches.

"'I'd think it was a miracle,' said the woman, 'if I didn't know that God takes no notice of old besoms like me.'

"The Pope's men looked at each other. Then they scraped away the earth beneath the thorn. Soon they uncovered Kenelm's little body and his head – and as they lifted them away from the earth, a spring of water bubbled up where they had been.

"The Pope's men set the head to the body's

neck, and they joined together again, leaving only a red line. Kenelm had not rotted at all. He looked as if he was sleeping.

"The Pope's men carried the body to the royal hall, and there they laid it before the throne where Askbert sat. Everyone knew that Askbert was the last man to be seen with the young king, and now people looked strangely at him.

" 'He was alive the last I saw him!' said Askbert. 'I know nothing of his death! Bring me bread!' And when bread was brought to him, he tore off a piece and said, 'If I killed my foster-son, Kenelm, may this piece of bread choke me!' He put the bread in his mouth, chewed, swallowed – and choked to death before the eyes of all who watched. No one tried to help him.

"Then Quendry was asked what she had to do with her brother's death. 'Nothing, I swear,' she said. 'If Askbert killed him, I knew nothing of it.'

"One of the Pope's men asked if she would swear that on the Bible. 'Bring me here a Bible,' she said, 'and I will swear it.'

"So they brought her a Bible, and she opened it and held it in her hands. 'If I had anything to do with my brother's death, may my eyes fall out of my head on to these pages!' And her eyes fell out of her head – splat! – on to the page. I am told that this Bible, with its spattered, bloody pages, is one of the treasures of Mercia. Maybe you've seen it, my lord?"

"I have seen the reliquary in which it is kept," said the abbot. "The book itself is not shown to everyone. Is the story finished?"

"Not quite. One of the Pope's men – a kindly sort, and pitying a beautiful woman, as kindly men do – took Quendry by the hand and led her to the spring of water that had risen where Kenelm's body had been buried. He got her to kneel beside the spring, and to pray for forgiveness while he bathed her eyeless sockets with the water – and her eyes grew back! Her sight was restored. So the first miracle performed by little Kenelm was to heal the sister who had wished him harm.

"The spring restored many, many others. A sip from it made the dumb speak. A little in the ear cured the deaf. Withered limbs were made whole and healthy. Pilgrims came from every part of these islands, and even from foreign parts, to drink and bathe in the waters of Saint Kenelm's spring.

"It may be that if you took me there, and

dipped my neck-end in it, the rest of me would grow back!"

"Is that what you want us to do?" asked the abbot.

"No. I want only to be taken to my king, wherever he is, so that I can keep my promise. My lord of the Christian men, you have heard me tell a tale of a Christian saint, while resting on a your Holy Book. Am I a danger to anyone? Is there any evil magic in me? I appeal to you, help me to reach my king."

The abbot looked thoughtful. "You can only exist by the grace of the power of God. It makes no sense that He would allow such grace to fall on a heathen. You must be a Christian. And a saint."

"I have never been a Christian," said Egil, the head. "I have always worshipped the True Gods, the Gods of my fathers."

"Then you must be a Christian without knowing it," said the abbot.

"How could that be?" asked the head.

"God's ways are not ours," said the abbot. "A man may be a witch and a tool of the Devil without knowing it. He may go about, meaning only to do good, and yet doing only harm, because the Devil is working through him. So a man might be a Christian without knowing it, his mind fixed on false gods, and yet bringing many to Christ, because God is working through him. And God has sent you to us, to draw pilgrims to us and help us in our work."

"I must go to my king!" cried the head.

"Perhaps," said the abbot. "In a little while. In time, when you come to your true self, you may help to convert him. But first, let us put my theory, and your miraculous powers, to the test."

A monk standing behind the abbot's chair leaned forward and whispered to him. "Indeed!" said the abbot. "The Lady Osyth."

"Who is she?" the head demanded.

"A sad lady. Afflicted with a sickness not of the body, but of the mind. She has not smiled or laughed for three years and truly, laughter is needful for health. Her father has begged us many times to cure her, but none of our prayers or medicines have been of any help. Could you, O miraculous head, make the lady laugh?"

"My stories are more often told to men than ladies, but – I know a few that have set folk laughing before now. What if I do make the lady laugh? Will you then give me to my king – or will I be locked up in a box here, in your

God-house, and asked to cure the lame and the blind?"

The abbot rapped his finger-ends on the wooden table. "I shan't send you to your king if you *don't* make the lady laugh," he said.

The head sighed. "Once," it said, "you would have been afraid to speak to me like that. But now the worst I can do is spit at you. Bring me to your sad lady, Christian man, and if I can make her laugh, I will."

4

The Head Tells a Story for Lady Osyth

"My daughter," said Thane Redwald, "is not used to such sights."

"The head could remain hidden," said the abbot. "I am sure I have no wish to shock or disgust the lady."

"Saint Egil?" said Redwald. "I've heard of no Saint Egil. The only Egil I've heard of was storyteller to King Penda. Is he dead yet?"

The abbot was startled. "Who? The storyteller?"

"King Penda. He was badly wounded, I hear."

"I have heard no news of his death," said the abbot. "I am sure he's being tended with the best of care."

"I doubt if our Edgar would weep if he died, though," said Redwald.

"I have come here," said the abbot firmly, "to cure your daughter's melancholy, if God be willing. With this holy relic." His hands rested on the oaken reliquary.

"That Egil the Storyteller," said Thane

Redwald. "He was a heathen and a bad lot."

"This is the head of that same Egil," the abbot admitted. "Moments before he died, he received Christ and became a Christian. There is more rejoicing in Heaven over one heathen converted than over ten Christians."

From inside the box came a muttering.

The abbot tapped lightly on the box's side. "A new saint is a great well-spring of God's power. I trust that this overflowing grace will cure the Lady Osyth where so much physic has failed."

"Aye," said Redwald, his arms folded. "And then the pilgrims will come tramping to your monastery, with coin and gifts." The muttering from inside the reliquary grew louder. "Have you rats in there?"

"It is Saint Egil's head," said the abbot. "Praying."

Redwald's eyes opened wider. "It talks? Let me hear!"

The abbot lifted the oak lid, and Egil's voice was suddenly loud in the room – "fat-headed arse!"

Redwald's face filled with astonishment and wonder as he realized the magical power held within the box. "Quickly!" he said. "Bring it to Osyth's bower – bring it now!"

✾ ✾ ✾

The Lady Osyth's bower was small, dark and hot. There were no windows, the door had been shut a long time, and the heat from the fire was stifling. The scent of lavender and cloves was so strong that, after a few breaths, the abbot's head ached.

Lady Osyth lay in a large, carved bed, its hangings drawn. When her father pulled them back, she raised her head from the pillow. Peering through long, tangled hair, she said, "There's a draught! Father! I think you were raised in a barn."

"You need some fresh air," said Thane Redwald. His daughter exclaimed, and threw herself back on her pillow. "I've brought some visitors to see you," he added.

"Not again!"

"Osyth! Manners! Here is Abbot Wilfred."

"Oh, not more prayers! I'm sick of prayers."

"The lady is poorly, she must be forgiven her annoyance," said the abbot. "Lady, I have brought with me a most precious relic of Saint Egil, which I hope may bring peace and healing to you."

The girl sat up in bed again, her face hidden

in hair. "A relic?" she said. "What bit is it? A finger?" She looked at the box. "Bigger than a finger. A hand? A knee?"

Holding the box before him, the abbot said, "It is the most blessed saint's head."

"Ooh!" said Osyth. "Let me see!"

"Osyth," said her father. "It is not a sight for you."

"I'm not afraid to see it," she said. "I'm a warrior's daughter, aren't I? When I'm older, I might have to search battlefields for your body and the bodies of my brothers, all hacked to bits."

"I pray you never shall," said her father.

"I may have to, you can't tell. I need to know what to expect. Bring it here and let me see!"

"I think it better –" said her father.

"If you don't let me see it, how can it do me any good? Anyway, if you don't let me see it, I shall put my fingers in my ears and sing, and not hear any prayers or sermons, and I shall never be cured."

Thane Redwald sighed and sat down on the edge of the bed. "Bring it here and let her see it," he said. "If it gives her nightmares, serve her right!"

The abbot brought the box to the bed and set

it down on the covers. Osyth leaned forward and scrabbled at her hair, pushing it back from her face and behind her ears, so she could see.

Lifting the lid of the box, the abbot took from it a bundle of linen, which he placed close to the girl. Parting the linen, he revealed the head.

"Oooh," Osyth said. She leaned close, peering at the head, eagerly inspecting every curl of its beard, every eyelash, every pore of its skin and every crease of its lips.

The head opened its eyes and said, "Boo!"

Osyth was so startled that her arms and her whole body lifted upwards. She gasped, and then wept, turning towards her father. "Oh, take it away! I don't like it!"

Her father put his arms round her, and glared at the abbot. "Laugh! I want her to laugh – she weeps enough!"

"I am sorry, deeply sorry –" the abbot began, but stopped when he saw that Osyth was already turning her head from her father's shoulder to see the head again.

"A warrior's daughter!" bawled the head, as if it was yelling to a whole army. "And she cries because I said boo!"

"You made me jump!" she said. "You're

cut-off. You're not supposed to talk."

"I'm a saint!" yelled the head. "Saint Egil, that's me! I can talk if I want."

Osyth let go of her father and leaned towards the head. "You're supposed to make me laugh," she said.

"And you think I can't?"

"Nobody else has been able to," she said. "I'm very sad. I'm close to the sin of despair."

"And what brought that on?" the head asked.

"Growing up," she said.

The head raised its brows. "That'll do it," it said. Then it raised its voice again. "Thane – if I make your daughter laugh, what will you do for me?"

"I will make a gift to the monastery," said the thane.

"No! What will you do for me? Can you keep a promise? Will you promise to have me taken to my king, Penda?"

The thane looked confused. "I have no power to make any such promise."

"How about you, lassie?" said the head to the Lady Osyth. "Do you keep promises? Shall I tell you a story about promises?"

"Oh, tell me a story, yes!" she said. "But I shan't laugh."

"Laugh or not, as you please," said the head. "Hark! Here is my story. . ."

✠ ✠ ✠

"There was a mouse. A wee, grey mousie running about on a broad table top, snatching up a crumb of bread here, a crumb of cheese there – until it ran against a wall, a tower, at the table's centre. It was a jug, lassie, a big wooden jug.

" 'What's in the jug?' thinks Mousie to himself, and he sets himself to clambering up the side of the jug – digging in his little claws – scrambling up until he reaches the top of the jug, the very lip. He leans over, nose twitching, taking a good sniff. It's ale! Good, rich ale. But Mousie, while he's leaning and sniffing, slips – and falls – sploosh! – into the jug.

"Under he goes and comes up spluttering – and starts swimming. Round and round he swims, and ever and again he tries to clamber out. But the inside of the jug's smoother than the outside, and wet and slippery. He can't get out. And he's getting tired. His little legs are aching. 'I'm going to die,' thinks Mousie. 'I'm going to drown'.

"But sauntering along the table comes a cat.

And, cats being curious, it sticks its head into the jug. And there it sees Mousie, splashing in the ale and clawing at the sides.

" 'Oh, Cat!' cries Mousie. 'Save me! Stick in your paw and scoop me out!'

" 'Oh no,' says the cat. 'I should get my paw wet and sticky. I don't like that.'

" 'But I shall drown!' says Mousie.

" 'What's that to me?' says the cat. 'You will drown and the people will come along and find you floating in their ale. They'll throw away you and the ale – and I shall eat you, flavoured with ale, without getting my paw wet, and without all the trouble of catching you. Good result for me.'

" 'Listen to me!' cries Mousie. He's tiring all the while and can't swim for much longer. 'Push over the jug! The ale will all spill and if you're quick to jump aside, you won't get wet.'

" 'But you'll run away,' says the cat, 'and I won't get to eat you. No, better for me to let you drown and wait for you to be tipped outside the door.'

" 'I won't run away!' cries Mousie. 'I promise! If you save me from drowning, I'll stay and let you eat me!'

"'Now why would you do that?' asks the cat.

" 'Because drowning is such a horrible death,' says the mouse. 'It's a poor, dank, coward's death, a fool's death. To die between the teeth of a cat – that, at least, is a mouse's death! That is the death a mouse is born for, an honourable death.'

" 'True,' says the cat. 'Every mouse should die in a cat's mouth.'

" 'I can tell my time is come,' says Mousie. 'This is the day fated for me to die. I accept it. But I would a thousand times rather die by cat than drown in a jug of ale. Help me, Cat! Push over the jug and save me from drowning, and I'll let you eat me!'

" 'Do you promise?' asks the cat.

" 'By all the Gods, I promise! Er – by the One and only Christian God, I promise! I give you my word, on a mouse's honour, on my tail, on my whiskers, I swear I will let you eat me.'

" 'Very well,' says the cat and, putting its paws against the jug, it tipped the jug over.

"Down on to the boards fell the jug with a bang! Out flowed the ale, carrying the mouse with it, in a rush, towards the table edge! Over the edge it carried him!

"With a spring, the cat jumped to the table's edge and looked over. There was the mouse, running as fast as he could across the floor – running like a good 'un.

" 'Come back!' cried the cat. 'You promised I could eat you! You promised!'

"The mouse reached the wall and its hole, but it stopped long enough to say, over its shoulder, 'Don't you know any better? Don't you know not to believe what anybody says when they're in drink?' And then it dived into its hole and was safe."

Thane Redwald laughed out loud. The abbot smiled, but as if he disapproved. Osyth shook her head, and her mouth pouted. "I don't think it's funny. It doesn't make sense."

"You're not to believe what anybody says *when they're in drink*, see?" her father said. "The mouse was in drink because it had fallen in the –" He broke off when he saw her sulky face.

"It's a silly story," she said.

"I agree," said the head. "A silly tale of a tail. But listen a little longer, lassie. The cat sat on the table's edge in a sulk, as you often see cats sit. Ah, poor disappointed cat. Embittered cat, that will not believe or trust in future, and will help no more mice – no, nor cats neither! This sad cat has learned that the most solemn promises can be broken.

"How much better for us all, brothers, if promises were never broken. How much better if, when man or woman made a promise, we could believe them and trust them – how trade would flourish, how friendships would grow, how much less disappointment and bitterness there would be in the world!"

"Now you're preaching at me," Osyth said. "I thought you were going to make me laugh. I told you that you wouldn't."

"But if I did make you laugh, lassie? Come here, lean close, let me whisper."

Osyth's eyes lit a little, and she bent closer to the head.

"It's not going to –?" said Thane Redwald uneasily. "It's not – it won't say anything – out of the way – to her?"

The abbot looked him up and down. "A saint's head! There is nothing unclean or improper in that head, I assure you!"

"Closer, closer," said the head to Osyth, and she brought her ear close to its mouth.

"Send me to my king!" whispered the head. "Will you promise to do all you can, if I make you laugh? Will you use all your smiles, and all your tears, all your sulks and all your flounces, to get old Egil sent to his king?"

Osyth drew back and looked at the head very seriously. She was flattered that it asked her help, and thought her capable of outwitting the abbot and ruling her father. "I promise," she said. "On my honour."

"On your beauty?" asked the head.

"On everything I value. But first you have to make me laugh."

"Time enough for that," said the head. "Thane Redwald!"

"What?" asked the man, startled to be so suddenly addressed.

"I often heard tell of you at King Penda's court."

"Of me?" said the thane. "I think not. Some other man, maybe."

"You are known," said the head, "as a thoughtful man, whose words are worth hearing?"

"Really? No, no, not me."

"Oh yes – but they do say, as well, that you're a man who likes a wager. Is that so?"

"It is you they tell of, Daddy," Osyth said.

"It's said that when horses are raced or fought," said the head, "you cannot hold back from betting. It's said you will bet on dice – or who can drink most – or which leaf will fall from a tree first."

Thane Redwald's face had become stiff, and he looked nervously at the abbot. "I never bet more than I can afford to lose."

"That I've heard, too," said the head. "Well, I have a wager for you."

The thane laughed. "I've bet with men who've lost their heads before – but never with one who'd lost his body!"

"Will you hear the wager?"

"I've never bet with a saint before!" said the thane, laughing again.

"Indeed, I think it little becomes a saint," said the abbot.

"And since when has a prayer-peddler told a saint what to do?" the head demanded. "Thane, will you hear the wager?"

The thane eyed the abbot nervously, but it could be seen from his face that he was longing to know. "Say on."

"It's simple. I wager that I can make you call me a liar."

The thane looked puzzled, then shook his head. "I don't understand."

"There's nothing hard," said the head. "I'll tell you a little about myself – I'll tell you about when I was a lad – and if you once call me a liar, then you lose."

Thane Redwald folded his arms. "All I've got to do is not call you a liar, no matter what you say, and I win?"

"That's all," said the head.

"Too easy."

"Oh, easy, easy," said the head.

"It could go on all day and all night!" said Osyth.

"You're right, lassie," said the head. "Thane, have you such a thing as an hour-glass?"

"No," said the thane. "But in a while, the cows will pass the door on their way to be milked. If I haven't called you a liar by then, I win. Do you agree?"

"Agreed," said the head. "And now the stakes. If I win, you, Thane Redwald, must do all you can to deliver me to my king. Agreed?"

"Agreed," said the thane, who didn't see how he could lose. "And if I win?"

"Oh, if you win, you may seal me in a Christian altar and call me a saint, or throw me on a dung-heap, stick me on a spike, throw me in a river, whatever you please."

"Not much to win," said the thane, "but – well, how many can say they've won a bet from a saint? I agree."

"Good," said the head. "Then I begin. . ."

*** ***

"This all happened," said the head, "at the time of the Great Famine—"

"What?" asked Thane Redwald. "Ten years ago?"

"No. The one last year."

"Well, well," said Redwald, "I have a long memory and I can't recall any great famine last year – but I'm sure you're right, my friend. I'll not call you a liar."

"I should think not, so early in the game. Anyway, at the time of the Great Famine last year, King Penda's country was in desperate trouble. Not a grain of wheat or rye or oat was to be had. The king would have sent ships abroad to trade for food, but as you'll remember, we were beset by gale after gale, that lifted the thatch off halls and blew down trees—"

"Your memory is far better than mine, friend head," said Redwald, laughing. "A year ago? I don't remember so much as a high wind."

"Are you calling me a liar?" the head asked.

"No, no, no. I'm getting older. I daresay my memory is not so sharp as it was."

"Because of the gales, not a ship could set sail," said the head. "And King Penda was in despair, thinking of his starving people. But I went to him and said, 'Don't you worry, King. Give me a couple of days – maybe three – and I'll be back with grain enough to fill every porridge pot in your kingdom and all your storehouses a dozen times over.'

"'How are you going to do that, Egil?' asks the king.

" 'Why, I shall climb to the top of our highest mountain, and take a good run up, and leap over the sea into some foreign country where they have plenty of grain – and then I shall leap back with it.' "

"A good plan", said Redwald, nodding. "Eh, sweetheart?"

"It's silly," Osyth said.

"I'm glad you don't think I was lying," said the head.

"Not at all, not at all."

" 'Egil,' said King Penda, 'we rely on you.' So off I went, determined to serve my king. I climbed to top of the highest mountain, and I made a few practice jumps, to limber up, and then I took a good long run and I leaped – I leaped right over the towns and saw all the little fields below me. I saw the sea passing beneath me with all the white tops to the waves. And I came down in – well, I didn't know where it was, but it was hot, very hot. And there were fields of corn on either side. So I walked along a bit, through the corn, until I met a man, and I said to him, 'Where am I, brother?' And he said to me, 'Rooshia.'"

"Oh, he could speak English, then?" Redwald asked.

"I had a stroke of luck there," said the head. "It turned out he was an Orkney chap who was travelling, but he'd been living there in Rooshia for a while."

"That was a stroke of luck," said Redwald.

"You're not calling me a liar, are you?" asked the head.

"Oh no. I understand Orkney men wander all over the world. After all, what is there to keep them at home?"

"I'll let that pass," said the head. "This chap's name was Thorgeir. We chatted about home for a while, and then I said, 'Who owns all this corn? Do you think he would give me some?'

"'It all belongs to the King of Rooshia,' said Thorgeir. 'I know him. I'll go with you and we'll ask him.'

"So we went to see the king, and told him all about the famine in King Penda's land, and asked him, would he give me some of his corn to take back with me?"

"Did the King of Rooshia speak English too?" Redwald asked.

"Don't be daft. Thorgeir could speak a bit of Rooshian, and he translated for me. Anyway, the upshot was that the king would let me have some grain, but not too much. He said I could have as much as I could cut myself, not with a scythe, but with a little bill-hook. You know what I mean by a bill-hook, Redwald?"

"I've done my share of work in the fields," Redwald said.

"How about you, lassie?" the head asked.

"I don't know and I don't care," Osyth said. "I'm getting bored."

"Bear up," said the head. "A bill-hook, lassie, is a little weeding hook with a wooden handle. You have to gather up every handful of grass or weeds – or corn – before you can cut it. Slow work. The king knew I wouldn't be cutting much corn with a bill-hook. But I showed him. I cut forty acres of his wheat."

"Forty acres!" said Redwald.

"In an hour," said the head.

"Forty acres in an hour! That was a day's work all right."

"Are you calling me a liar?" asked the head.

"Not at all. I'm sure that the good abbot believes it as much as I do."

"I'll tell you how I did it," said the head. "I went out to the fields with the bill-hook in my hand, determined to cut as much as I could, though I knew I had my work cut out. I'd hardly started – I'd hardly cut more than a couple of handfuls – when out of the corn ran a brown hare. Well, I'm partial to stewed hare, so I thought, 'I'll just catch that hare before I get stuck in, and it'll make a dinner for me in a few day's time'. So I ran after the hare – and I can run when I put my mind to it – and I almost caught the hare—"

"You almost caught a hare, on foot?" said Redwald.

"Why, don't you believe me?"

"Oh, every word," said Redwald.

"I'd almost caught it when it got its second wind and put on a spurt of speed and drew away from me – so I flung the bill-hook at it. And the bill-hook whirled through the air and the wooden handle stuck in the hare's arsehole—"

"Language!" cried Redwald, looking at his daughter.

Osyth said, "That's cruel! And rude!"

"And pretty unbelievable," said the head.

"Oh, I believe it," said Redwald. "Believe me, I believe it."

"Away the hare ran, round and round the field, and into the next field and the one after – and every stalk of corn it passed, it cut down, with the bill-hook stuck in its arse-hole. Up and down, round and round – forty acres of wheat that hare cut, in an hour."

"I never heard the like," said Redwald.

"Are you calling me a liar?" asked the head.

"No, no."

"Well, since I'd stuck the bill-hook in the hare's arsehole, the Rooshian King had to allow that – in a way – I'd cut it. But, he said to me, 'How are you going to carry all this wheat home with you?'

"'Never you worry,' I said. 'I'll think of a way.' And just then, I felt something bite me. I put my hand inside my shirt, and caught a flea. So I killed the flea, and skinned it, and I packed every last grain of the wheat the hare had cut into the flea's skin."

Redwald grinned. "You packed the grain from forty acres of wheat into a flea's skin."

"Why, aye. I'm good at packing. Are you calling me a liar?"

"No, no. I wanted to be clear, that's all. You packed it all into a flea's skin. And how did you carry it home?"

"Ah, now that's where things started being troublesome," the head said. "I heaved the flea-skin on to my back and I set off on the way home but, though I'm a strong man, I'll tell you the truth—"

"Oh, you'll tell us the truth?" asked Redwald.

"Are you calling me a liar?"

"Never, never shall I call you a liar," said Redwald.

"I'll tell you the truth, I found that load a bit hard to carry. I tried it on one shoulder, then the other. I humped it along until I was sweating gobs of dripping. I dragged it behind me, but it was no better. It was too much for me. And I almost wept, to think I should have to let my king down, that was depending on me. But just then a flock of geese went over. To start with, I thought it was a thunderstorm, the sky darkened so much. And then I thought night was coming. But I heard the geese honking and their wings beating as they came lower and lower. And the leader called out to me: 'Egil Grimmssen! Well met! Are you in a bit of trouble, lad?'"

"The geese spoke to you?" asked Osyth.

"What's so strange about that? I'm speaking to you now, aren't I?"

"So you are," said Redwald. "We're sorry for interrupting you again. The geese spoke to you. Go on."

" 'I've got to get this sack back to England, to Penda's land, in the next couple of days,' I said. 'And I don't know how I'm going to do it, because it's too heavy for me to carry.'

"'Don't worry about that,' says the goose leader. 'We'll help you out.' And they all came down to land, and they all hutched up together, to make a wide, feathery platform of geese. 'Get up on our backs,' they said. 'We'll fly you home.'

"So I humped and dragged and heaved the flea-skin sack up on to their backs, and I lay down beside it, and I was so tired, and their feathers were so soft and warm that I fell straight off to sleep. And when I woke up, hours later, it was so peaceful. There was blue sky and warm sun above me, and the sound of beating wings and rushing air, and now and again, the cry of a goose. I rolled over and parted the goose-feathers and peered down and I could get a glimpse – like peeking through a key-hole – of dark clouds, and then the sea far below, and little ships being tossed in the gales. I was over the North Sea, and I could see the shore of England, of King Penda's land – and very glad I was to see it.

"But I could hear all the geese cackling and honking and carrying on with a terrible din, and then the leader cries out, 'Oh, Egil – it's too heavy! We can't carry it any further! We're done in. We shall have to let you go!' And they all flew away from under me and let me, and the flea's skin and all the corn—"

"They let it all fall?" said Redwald.

"That's the way of it."

"I would have thought after carrying you and the corn all the way from Rooshia, they could have managed a couple more wing-beats to bring you home," said Redwald.

"I get the feeling you're calling me a liar," said the head.

"Put it out of your mind. I'm not."

"Down I came like – like thunder," said the head. "Me, the flea-skin – it split – and all the corn. Rattling and roaring through the air. Like a hail-storm. And me the biggest hailstone of the lot. Down to the earth with a crash."

"Were you killed?" asked Redwald.

"Are you calling me a liar?"

"I was asking a simple question, that's all."

"I thought I would land in the sea, but I looked down and saw that I was going to thump on to the land after all. And I could see some nice, soft fields that I knew were near the king's hall, and I was hoping I would land there, but no. I landed on a big, hard rock."

"And were you killed then?" asked Redwald.

"Are you calling me a liar?"

"Touchy."

"I wasn't killed, but I went into that rock up to my neck and I couldn't get out. I could move my head from side to side and look about—"

"You must have looked then much as you do now," said Redwald.

"An unkind and unnecessary comment, Thane, if I might say so," said the head.

"I am sorry," said Redwald.

"I could look about, and I could see all the grain I'd brought from Rooshia lying all over the land, heaped up, metres thick. It had all showered out of the sky like yellow snow. And the birds were coming and eating it. That made me mad. I wanted to jump up and chase them off, but I couldn't get out of the rock. What could I do?"

"I'm sure you're going to tell us," said Redwald.

"Well, a man came riding by, one of the king's house-carls, with a sword at his side. He'd been caught in the shower, and had corn in his hat and on his shoulders and in all the folds of his clothes. And he was riding along, staring open-mouthed at all the corn everywhere. And I shouted to him. 'Over here! Over here!'

"He came and looked at me and said, 'You're the king's storyteller.'

"'I know I am!' I said.

"'What are you doing in that rock?' he said.

"'I fell out of the sky,' I said, 'and now I'm stuck. Do me a favour, will you? Draw your sword and cut off my head.'

"'I should get into awful trouble for doing that,' he said.

"'Do it!' I said. 'Do it now! Do as I say! Do it!' And I shouted so loud, and got so red in the face, that he was scared, and he drew his sword and whacked my head off, just as I told him."

"You seem to make a habit of getting your head cut off," said Redwald.

"Oh? Are you calling me a liar?"

"I was just saying."

"Anyway, my head at least was free. So my head ran off to the king's hall—"

"How, exactly, did your head run by itself?" asked Redwald.

"Are you calling me a liar?"

"Not that."

"My head rolled. It rolled along the ground. Are you happy now? But as my head rolled along through the heaps of the corn, a fox came trotting by. Now this was a hardened, wicked fox, a vixen, that had been robbing the royal hen-houses for a year or more. And it sees my head and thinks it a nice morsel! So the fox chases my head! And I'm watching from the rock where I'm trapped, and I can see the fox catching up, and I'm shouting, 'Run, head! Run, run!' "

"Forgive me asking," said Redwald, "but how did your body watch from the rock, and how did your body shout, when your head was rolling in front of the fox?"

"You're not calling me a liar, are you?"

"Never let it be said."

"Well, the fox was getting closer and closer to my head, and snapping at it with its teeth, and I was getting more and more excited and het-up as I watched until I got so worked up that the heat of me cracked the rock and out I jumped! And I ran after that fox – and the fox caught my head in its teeth – and I ran faster yet, and I caught up with that fox, and I kicked it, and kicked it and kicked it, and I kicked seven young foxes out of that fox, and I kicked seven colours of shit out of each of those young foxes and you know what?"

"What?" asked Redwald.

"Why the worst fox's worst shit was worth more than you and the abbot lumped together."

"You're a liar!" Redwald shouted; and, "You're a liar!" cried the abbot. And the Lady Osyth fell back on the bed, laughing so hard that she bounced, laughing so hard that she tossed about and cried.

"And never a cow has passed the door or mooed," said the head. "I win. Pay your wager."

"That was no win!" said Thane Redwald. "You cheated!"

"No man need honour a wager won by trickery," said the abbot. "Besides, this relic of Saint Egil is in my keeping."

"Don't take him away, Father Abbot!" said the Lady Osyth. "I want to hear him tell more stories. I shall be sad again if I don't."

She looked as if she was going to cry, and

her father's face was even more unhappy.

"I need not start back to the monastery today," said the abbot.

"I shall need to hear many stories," said the lady to her father, "if I am to stay cheerful. Many, many stories."

"I might stay as long as a week," said the abbot.

"It would be better if Saint Egil was left with us," said Lady Osyth. "For good. Wouldn't it, Father? Wouldn't it? We could look after him."

"We shall see," said Thane Redwald, which made his daughter quickly put her hands to her face, hiding her mouth. "Don't pester the good abbot now, Sythie. We can settle things later."

"Of course, Father," said Osyth. She looked at the head of the storyteller, and winked.

5

THE HEAD TELLS OF
UNCANNY THINGS

"Tell me a lovely story," said Osyth, rolling on the bed. "It doesn't have to make me laugh."

She was alone with the head in her bower. Two candles burned, casting a warm, grainy light, and leaving deep shadows under the rafters and in corners. The head was set on a wooden chest beside the bed, lying in a pewter dish of dull silver, its red hair and beard about it. "I think you have little trouble in laughing, lassie," said the head, "when your father isn't looking or listening."

She turned her smile into her hands. "Maybe."

"You know how to make him dance to your tune."

"It's good for him," she said. "Now tell me a story. Don't keep me waiting."

"You keep me waiting. When will I see my king?"

"If you want me to make Daddy dance, you

have to give me time. I can get round him, but not all in a moment."

The head sighed. "A story that doesn't have to make you laugh. A story about a girl like you, eh?"

"That would do very well."

"A girl not so much like you. This girl worked for a living."

"What did she do?" Osyth asked.

"She was a serving-girl on a farm. She did all the things that you only think of if they aren't done – by somebody else. Up in the morning, she was, before it was light, to fetch heavy pails of water, and stir up the fires, and milk the goats and make the breakfast—"

"I could do all that," Osyth said. "Well, I've never milked a goat, or made breakfast—"

"Or any other meal," said the head. "Or carried a pail of water, or tended a fire."

"I could learn!" Osyth cried.

"To be sure you could, lassie, but you'd be exhausted, and you'd whinick about getting dirty and getting blisters – and my serving-girl's work had hardly started! She must feed the fowl, and air the beds, and get the dinner on, and scour the pots, and grind corn, and feed the pigs, and mend clothes, and milk the goats again – oh, and if she had a minute, she must spin thread – but she never had a minute. While she was running after one job another one was catching her up. But she wasn't exhausted! Oh no! Thora – that was her name, I knew her well at one time—"

"Was she your sweetheart?" Osyth asked, and giggled at the thought of a head – nothing but a head – having a sweetheart.

"Ah, other days, other times," said the head. "I knew her well, that's all I'll say. But Thora thrived on all the work. Her master and mistress worked her hard, but fed her well, and she was a big, bonny girl, with a fine head of thick, wavy hair—"

Osyth threw herself back on the bed, her arms folded. "Well, what happened to her, this Thora?"

"It happened one day she'd been sent out to look for straying sheep. So she cantered along the lanes, running, then walking, then running again, and keeping a quick eye out for any chance to gossip, when she passed the grave-yard. Some men were digging a grave. So over she went, to ask them if they'd seen the sheep – but really to ask them whose grave they were digging, and to chat, and to flirt."

"Talking to men!" said Osyth.

"Oh, she never missed a chance to talk to men, that one. And the men saw her coming, and straightened up with grins, because they knew Thora, and they knew they'd have a few laughs with her."

"She sounds a minx to me," Osyth said.

"And that's where you're wrong. She was a good, kind, warm, friendly girl. 'Looking for a man, Thora?' says one of the grave-diggers. 'Look what we've found here.' And he points to a heap of old bones they'd thrown out of the grave.

"'A big lad, whoever he was,' says the other digger. And it was a big skull, half as big again as any ordinary skull. There were the thigh-bones too, great long thigh-bones.

"'Ooh, lovely long legs,' says Thora, and she picks up the skull and holds it in front of her."

"Urgh!" Osyth pulled her mouth awry. "She picked up the skull? You're bad enough, and you still have a face!"

"Ah, but remember, Madam Finick, Thora had put her hands into all sorts of muck – gutting rabbits and chickens, cleaning up after babies and drunken men. She wasn't fussy. She held the skull up in front of her, and said, 'If this one was still above ground, I swear I'd give him a great, big kiss!'

"'I'm still above ground, Thora!' says one of the grave-diggers.

"'Ah, but you're not a big lad, you're just a little shrimp!'

"'Oh, good things come in small packages!'

"The other grave-digger stretched himself up tall, showing off that he was a finger's breadth taller than his mate.

"'Too old for me, I'm just a young thing!' said Thora.

"'Many a sweet tune's been played on an old pipe', said the grave-digger.

"'And many an old pipe's out of tune!' And Thora threw the big skull down and flounced off, laughing, to find the sheep.

"She found the sheep, and brought it home, and gossiped with others she met on the way, and reached home with lots of news to make the evening merry, and never gave the old bones another thought. When the work was done, and the rush-dips lit, her master and mistress and the other servants were happy to listen to her chatter as she dished up food and passed it round. She was well thought of in the household, was Thora.

"As soon as the food was finished, they went to bed. They had no candles to burn, lassie, and they'd worked hard all day. They didn't have their own bowers and halls, either, but all bedded down in the one room, around the fire."

"Cosy," Osyth said.

"Crowded," said the head. "Thora was the last to bed, because it was her job to bank down the fire, so it would stay alight until morning, and snuff out all the rush-lights. But she slid under her blankets at last, and was ready to drop asleep at once – only she heard her name called. She lifted up her head. From outside – from the dark outside – came a voice calling, 'Thora!'"

"Oh!" Osyth drew up her knees and folded her arms in close to her body. "You should never answer when your name's called from outside at night! Didn't she know that?"

"But it's hard not to answer when your name's called. She listened, but she could only hear snoring from inside the house. So she laid her head down again and, just as she was dozing – 'Thora!' called the voice. 'Thora, come to me!'

"She lifted herself up on one elbow and

listened for a long time, but heard nothing. So then she said, softly, not to wake anyone, 'Is somebody there?' And she listened again. But there was no answer.

"She laid herself down to sleep a third time. And this time there came a tap at the house door, so loud it seemed to tap on her heart and set it swinging. 'Thora! Thora!' So she got up out of bed—"

"Oh, she's not going to go outside, is she?" Osyth cried. "Not outside in the dark?"

"She had to be sure," said the head. "Was she dreaming, or was someone outside calling for her? Dressed in nothing but her shift, she groped about by the dim red light of the banked fire, and found one of the rush-dips. She held it to the red turfs until it burned, and that gave her the faintest, weariest light – far, far dimmer than your beeswax candles, lassie – but enough to bring a little comfort. To the door she went, lifted the latch and dragged it open. Oh, but it was black as pitch outside, and the air was cold! The very touch of it made her shudder.

"No moon was shining, and the old farm-yard might as well have been a deep, dark hole. Against that darkness, the feeble little glimmer of the rush-dip was no light at all. 'Is anyone there?' She meant to say it boldly, but it came out a little squeak.

"Out of the darkness came a voice. It said, 'Come here to me, Thora. Come here.'"

"Oh, she's not going to go?" Osyth said. "I'd run back to bed. And hide under the covers!"

"But then the voice would go on calling and calling, all night. And the next night, and the next. Thora had to know who it was, and why they called. She sheltered the dim little rush-light with her hand, and took one step out into the darkness. The damp, muddy earth of the yard was cold to her feet, but she took another step.

"'Ah, come, Thora,' said the voice.

"'Who are you?' she said, but it didn't answer. She took another step, and another, and then something large and black loomed up, blocking her way, and making her gasp. She poked the rush-dip at it, and made out a rough-woven tunic, all muddy and dirty—"

"Oh no!" said Osyth.

"She lifted the rush-dip higher, and it lit the bristling hair of a beard – but a beard with mud and glistening worms caught in it."

"No!" said Osyth.

"Higher still Thora raised the rush-dip, and lit a grey face; a hollowed, grey, damp face, and two grey eyes gleaming dully at her from deep hollows and drooping lids.

"Thora stared, with not a word to say, but the man said, 'Ah, Sweet Thora, faded and gone is my ruddy complexion; Death has laid me low. My breath is strong now, and grimy are my whiskers – but do you remember what you said, Thora? That if I were above ground, you would give me a kiss? Here I am!' And the dead man spread wide his long arms."

Osyth, lying on the bed, covered her face with her hands.

"Would you kiss him, lassie?"

"No!"

"Would you kiss me, who you know?"

"Never!"

"Thora stood on tiptoe and said, 'Bend down, you tree, bend down!' And the ghastly grave-dweller bent down, so she could reach. Thora plucked a worm from his beard, and planted a kiss on his cold lips. 'There!' she said. 'Now let me sleep!' And she ran back to the house and her warm bed."

"To kiss a dead man!" Osyth shuddered as she lay on the bed. "I couldn't! I could never!"

"A brave, bold girl was Thora," said the head. "She paid her debts and she kept her promises. You're not alone in asking how she could do it. When she told of her night's adventure, the whole household asked her the same thing. 'That was the only man I ever kissed,' she said, 'who I can be sure won't go running after some other woman. Who else would he find to kiss him?'

"And ever after that Thora had extraordinary luck. Whatever she turned her hand to, she did well. Whatever plans she made, worked out. She married a man devoted to her, and she and her husband prospered. They had five healthy children, who all grew up to be highly thought-of. Thora never had a day's sickness and was a fine-looking woman even in old age. People said that she had something watching over her – and many thought it was the man she'd met that night, in the yard. She died suddenly one day, in her son's house. She was sitting by the fire when she looked up, smiled as if delighted, murmured something, and was dead, all in a moment. Those sitting nearest her said that her last words had been, 'Why – hello!'"

"What had she seen?" Osyth asked.

"How can anyone tell?" the head said. "She was dead, and couldn't be asked. What do you think she saw?"

"The dead man!" Osyth said.

"Aye," said the head. "Most folk thought that, after many years of faithful service, her dead lover had come to claim her as his own, and fetch her home."

"Is that the end?" Osyth asked.

"That's the end, yes."

"Well. . ." Osyth pulled strands of hair out of her tight plaits as she thought. "It was a little bit romantic, but. . . Too many bones and graves and worms! Yuck! No, it was horrible. I didn't like it at all."

"You said the story didn't have to make you laugh."

"It didn't have to be disgusting! Tell me another. A nice one, this time, with a happy ending."

"A love story? Is that what you're wanting?"

"There can be love in it," said Osyth. "Come on, tell me one I enjoy, and I'll really set my mind on how I can get you to your king."

"I'll tell you about some people I knew once, at home," said the head. "There was a farmer, and every summer he sent his sheep and cattle up to the sheiling—"

"That's a hut in the hills, isn't it?" said Osyth. "Where they send the herds for the summer grass."

"Very good," said the head. "You're wiser than you look."

"I shall have to manage my own household when I'm older, when I'm married. I have to know these things."

"Oh, you're going to be married, are you?"

"Tell the story," said Osyth.

"Every summer he had his sheep and cattle driven up to the sheiling, where they could spend the whole summer growing fat on the meadow grass up there. And he sent a shepherd and a cowman with them, and a dairymaid, to milk the herd every day and turn the milk into butter and cheese. Well, he had a daughter, this farmer, and she started going up to the sheiling as a little lass. At first, there was another woman with her, but the girl was so capable that soon she could manage by herself. And she was a quiet sort of girl. Never had much to say, and was happy enough to be alone. She said she looked forward to the long, quiet days in the hills.

"But she was a handsome girl—"

"What was her name?" Osyth asked.

"Katla. She was tall and strong, and her hair fell down to her knees. When it was made up into plaits, they were as thick as my arm – well, as thick as my arms were, when I had arms. And because she was beautiful and healthy, skilful and thrifty, the old farmer soon found many young men coming to his door and chatting about this and that, asking after his health and whether he needed any help about the farm. Well, it didn't take the old man long to catch on, and one evening, when they were sitting by the farmhouse fire, he asked Katla if she'd given any thought to marriage.

" 'Yes,' she said.

" 'And what are you thinking?' her father asked.

"She smiled. 'I'm thinking that I shall never get married.'

" 'What, never? What shall you do, then?'

" 'I shall go on as I am,' she said.

" 'But, daughter, things change, as quickly as the clouds in the sky or the water in the stream. I am growing old, and shan't be able to manage the farm as well as I used to. And one day I shall die, and you'll be left alone. It would be better if you had a husband when that day comes.'

" 'Not so,' she said. 'You know very well that I can manage the farm without any guidance. And we're not so poor that we can't hire a man to help with the heavy work.'

" 'Aye,' said the old man, 'but better still to have a man who'll do the heavy work for love.'

" 'Or his own profit,' said Katla. 'Father, look about you. There are men who marry a girl like me for her property, and then fribble it away on gambling, or fancy clothes, or drink. And if their wife objects, they punch her. Or they nag her into despair, until she's ready to drown herself.'

" 'Not all men are like that, Katla,' said her father.

" 'No, not all. You aren't. But often a woman can't tell what kind of man she's got until she's married to him; and then she's trapped.' "

"Oh, that's true!" Osyth said.

" 'But lassie,' said the old farmer to his daughter, 'you'll be so lonely.'

" 'I'm used to my own company and happy with it,' said Katla. 'Better to be alone and contented than wedlocked and miserable.'

" 'But what about children?' asked the farmer. 'Most women want children.'

" 'There are always children who need care,' said Katla. 'Orphans and children who come from families too big to keep them. If I ever find myself longing for a child, I can always take in one of them.'

"And nothing could change her mind. The young men kept on coming to the farm, but Katla was never more than polite to any of them, and mostly they were left to talk to her old father, which was not what they had come for. And Katla went on going with the herds to the summer sheiling, and taking more and more interest in the running of the farm, until she knew everything about it. So a couple more years passed.

"It was winter again, and the people were spending much of their time cooped up together in the house. The old farmer thought that his daughter was looking thicker through her middle than she ever had before – still, he thought nothing of it at first. But as time went on, she grew thicker and thicker, and started loosening the strings of her apron – and he caught her being sick a few times too.

" 'Katla,' he said to her. 'I think you're going to have a child.' "

"Was she?" asked Osyth.

"She said, 'How can you say such a thing – and you my father!'

" 'But you're getting so fat,' he said.

" 'I eat too much and sit about all day. I'll lose it when I can go to the sheilings.'

" 'But you've been sick,' he said.

" 'My belly was upset. I'll be better when we can eat fresh food. I'll be better at the sheilings, you'll see.'

" 'I don't think you should go to the sheilings,' he said, because he didn't believe her, and he thought that, if she was going to have a child, she would be better at the farm, where neighbours could come to help her.

" 'I shall go to the sheilings,' she said. 'I certainly shan't spend the summer as well as the winter shut up here!'

"He couldn't persuade her and, as she was angry whenever he tried to talk to her about her swelling belly or the sheilings, he soon stopped trying. But when the time for the sheilings came, he spoke to the cowman and the shepherd who were to go with her. 'I want you to keep an eye on my daughter,' he said. 'Don't leave her alone at any time, whatever you do.' They liked the old man, and were fond of Katla, and they promised.

"So off Katla went to the sheilings, as usual."

"And was she with child?" Osyth asked.

"Why don't you listen and find out?" said the head. "Katla and the two men trudged up to the hut in the hills, driving the sheep and cattle with them, and the nearer they came to the hut, the more Katla smiled. When they reached the hut, she set about cleaning the place up, and hummed and sang as she worked. 'It's been a while since we've known you so lively, Katla!' the cowman said to her, and she said,

"'Oh, I'm just so glad to be here again, out in the air and sun!'

"During the next few days, they each got on with their own work, just as in other years—"

"What did they do?" Osyth asked.

"What, have you never been to a sheiling, lassie? Well, the men looked over the animals, that had been shut up in sheds all winter, and led them to and from the best pastures, helped with the lambing and calving, and that meant sitting up all night sometimes. They looked out for eagles, helped Katla with the milking and sometimes with the butter and cheese-making. Making butter can be hard work, all that pounding away in a churn... And Katla was busy boiling water and scouring all the dairy equipment and keeping it clean, because dairy stuff has to be clean, or the butter's tainted. And she cooked for them, too – only simple stuff, like groats, that she could leave simmering all day. But there were hours and hours when there was nothing much to do except sit in the sun. The men caught fish, or snared rabbits – and they kept an eye on Katla, as they promised to do. There was always one of them in sight of her, or hanging round the hut. She never seemed to notice or care.

"Then, one morning, when they went yawning out of the hut into the thin, cool sunlight, they saw that the meadows were empty. Not a sheep nor a cow to be seen. So, whatever their promises, the cowman and the shepherd had no choice but to leave Katla alone while they looked for the animals.

"But it was strange weather. As they searched, a thick mist came down, and they lost themselves and each other. They had to wrap themselves in their cloaks and sit and wait for the mist to lift – because one thing you must always remember, lassie, is never to go blundering about on mountains in a fog. You might find a way down quicker than you think."

"If ever I find myself on a mountain in a fog, I shall be sure to remember," Osyth said.

"Don't laugh!" said the head. "We never know what may come to us. The richest little girl with the dotingest daddy may find herself alone on a mountain-side in a mist one day."

"Yes, but what about Katla?"

"Oh, Katla was left alone in the little sheiling hut, and she occupied herself somehow. When the fog lifted at last, and the men found the animals and came trudging back, tired and cold, they found her standing at the hut door, calling out, 'Hurry up! There's a hot meal waiting for you!' And she laughed. Indeed, she laughed a lot, at every little thing, in a giddy way that made them ask if she was all right.

" 'Oh, I'm very well,' she said. 'I'm glad to see you back safely – and glad that the fog's gone!' And she laughed again. It was odd – and they noticed something else as she moved about, filling their bowls—'

"What?"

"Her bulging belly had gone. She was as slim as she'd ever been."

"She'd had the baby!" Osyth said.

"Or she'd never been with child at all, just as she'd always said."

"She'd had the baby, and murdered it, and buried its body!" Osyth said. "And its little ghost will come and stand by her bed—"

"No, that's another story," said the head. "Let me tell this one. When the summer was over, everyone at the sheiling went back down to the farm. The old farmer had been looking out for them for days and, as soon as he saw them coming, he walked out to meet them, so keen was he to see his daughter again. As soon as he laid eyes on her, he saw that she was slim as a grass-blade. So he found the first chance he could to talk with the cowman and the shepherd. 'I asked you to keep a close eye on my daughter,' he said. 'Did you?'

" 'We tried,' said the shepherd. 'We tried our hardest. But one day all the animals were missing and we had to look for them.'

" 'And a fog came up,' said the cowman.

" 'We were away for a whole day,' said the shepherd. 'Sorry.'

" 'And when we got back, she was as you see her now.'

" 'I see,' said the old farmer, and he looked so sad and serious that she shepherd asked him what was the matter. 'I think,' he said, 'that my daughter knows the hills and the things that live in the hills better than you two will ever do. And I think I'd better get her married as soon as may be.'

" 'Good luck to you with that!' said the cowman, and the shepherd laughed, for they had eyes, and they'd seen the string of young men coming to the house and going away with no more than a smile for their trouble.

"But we know this, don't we, lassie – that if all the young women were hares on the mountain, all the young men would turn hounds on the scent!"

Osyth sang, "If all the young women were fish in the ocean, all the young men would turn gulls on the wing!"

"Aye. So it wasn't long after that another young man came calling at the farmer's house. He asked most politely after the old man's health, and about all the doings on the farm. Then he said, 'You know me, and you know no one has anything against me. And you know I come of a good family.'

" 'Indeed,' said the old man, who had heard things like this said a good many times by now. But this time it was different. This time he was determined to do more than listen and nod.

" 'You'll know that my father died last spring,' said the young man.

" 'Aye, and sorry I was to hear it. He was a good man.'

" 'The farm is mine now,' said the young man. 'I'm making a pretty good job of it, I think.'

" 'So I've heard,' said the old man.

" 'My mother keeps house for me, but she says she's getting too old to do it all, and she'd be glad to see me settled with a wife, and she'd like some grandchildren before she dies.'

" 'May the Gods grant her wish,' said the old man.

" 'So I've been looking around and thinking,' said the young man, 'and I've decided that I couldn't do better than to ask for your daughter as my wife.'

" 'And she'd walk a long way and not find a better husband,' said the old farmer. 'So, agreed! Let's talk about the settlement.'

" 'Aren't you going to ask your daughter?' the young man said.

" 'Don't worry, I'll see that she doesn't turn you down like all the others.' So they talked terms and the young man went away happy. Then the old man tackled Katla.

"They argued for days. The rest of the

household hardly dared lift their eyes above their plates. Most of the time they sneaked off into the barns and outhouses, looking for work to do – anything – that would keep them out of the way.

" 'I don't want to marry!' Katla said. 'I certainly don't want to marry a man I've hardly met! I won't do it!'

" 'And do you think, Madam,' her father demanded, 'that the story of your trip to the sheilings won't get out? How you were big as a cow in calf and came down light? How many will be lining up to marry you when that tale does the rounds?'

" 'But I don't want to marry!' Katla shouted.

" 'You don't want this, you don't want that – I'm through listening to your whims and fancies! I'm going to see you married to a good man before I die, like a father should, and that's that!'

" 'I'm not going to marry anyone!'

" 'Then you can walk over to his farm and explain to him and his mother why you're making a liar out of me, and what's wrong with him that he's not good enough for you!'

" 'You made the settlement without asking me!' Katla screamed back. 'You can go and tell them!'

The old man threw himself down on a bench with folded arms. 'I'm not budging!'

"Oh, it was a terrible row. It raged on and on, with pots being banged down, and spoons being thrown, until everybody's head was aching and everybody's hair was on end. Things got even worse, because one night the old farmer caught Katla trying to sneak out of the house with a bundle of clothes. He dragged her back in by her hair, and beat her with his hands, which no one had ever known before. 'You're not going!' he shouted. 'You'll stay here and marry a man!' Those who overheard thought this was an odd thing to say. The old man locked Katla in the food-store, which was the only room with a lock, and set men to watch her, and sent others to fetch the young man he'd chosen to marry her. No one could believe the old man was being so hard on the daughter he had always doted on.

" 'You must marry her now,' he said, when the young man came, 'or you'll never marry her.'

" 'I want a willing wife,' the young man said. 'Not one I have to lock up.'

Then the old man took him aside and whispered certain things which he suspected. 'You'll be saving her,' he said. 'And treat her well after you're married, and she'll come round.'"

"Saving her from what?" Osyth asked. "What did the old man suspect?"

"Listen and find out," said the head. "The young man didn't like it, but he agreed. They had witnesses and all that was necessary for a wedding, so they fetched Katla from the store-room. When she came up to the young man, she said to him, 'Since you are wedding me against my will, promise me one thing.'

"'What?' he asked.

"'When we are wed,' she said, 'if men should come to the farm over the winter, asking for work, never hire any of them without first asking me. Will you promise me that?'

"'It's an odd thing to ask,' said the young man. 'Why does it matter?'

"'Do you promise me?'

"'All right,' he said. 'I promise that I will never hire men over the winter without first asking your permission.'

"'If you break that promise, you'll be sorry for it,' she said.

"He clasped her hands and, smiling, said, 'I shall never break it.' He saw no reason why he ever should.

"So a wedding feast was held, though a bit of a hurried one, and the new wife went home with her husband. Her mother-in-law welcomed her, and handed her all the keys, and made it clear that she wouldn't interfere. 'It's your house now, my dear,' she said. 'I'll be glad to take things easier – but if you ever want my advice, you only have to ask.'

"Katla had managed a farm for most of her life, and she only had to ask a few questions about where things were kept. She took up management of the house very smoothly, and was a good manager too – but not a happy one. She hardly ever smiled, and was always cold towards her husband though he, poor man, bent himself out of shape to please her, and tried to have every dirty, heavy or unpleasant job done for her. 'I can do that perfectly well,' she would say, picking up a heavy bucket, or taking up a fork to muck out a pen. 'I want no favours, thank you.' Cold as ice, she was and, though living in the midst of a crowded farm-house, where everyone slept in the one room, she kept herself to herself.

"When spring came, everyone expected Katla to go up to the sheilings, but she said, 'I shall go to the sheilings no more. Let someone

115

else do it.' And she stayed at home. Ah, but when haymaking began, she would go out to the fields with everyone else, wouldn't she? No, she didn't. She stayed indoors and cooked for the haymakers, and spun thread and knitted, to pass the time. Her mother-in-law stayed with her because, as she said, 'I wouldn't be much use in the hay-fields these days.'

"After a while, the older woman grew tired of the heavy silence, and she started to tell stories, to pass the time and to hear a voice. She told tales of people she had known when she was a young woman, and of things she'd done, and stories she'd been told by her mother and grandmother. She feared she might be talking to herself, but quickly came to feel that her daughter-in-law was listening, though she said nothing.

" 'My mouth's dry now,' said the old woman, after an hour or so. 'I went to the garden to pick a bit of thyme. I've told my tale, now thee tell thine!'

" 'I don't know any,' said Katla.

" 'Oh, you must know one!'

" 'None.'

" 'Well, I think it a very poor thing,' said the old woman, 'that you've sat and enjoyed my stories, and now you won't tell me even one.'

"'If I know none, I know none,' said Katla. But then she seemed to feel sorry for being so short, and after a few moments of silence, she said, 'I know one, only one.'

"'Tell it, then.'

"'You won't like it – it isn't very long or very good.'

"'Let me be the judge.'

"'Once upon a time,' said Katla, 'there was a girl who went often to the sheilings in the summer, to be dairymaid. Not far from the hut there were some cliffs, and in those cliffs there lived an elf-man.'

"'An elf-man!' said the old woman. 'Did she see him?'

"'She saw him often.'

"'Oh! Was he very ugly?'

"'He wasn't ugly at all,' said Katla. 'He was tall, strong and beautiful.'

"'I thought elves were crooked and ugly – nasty things!' said the old woman.

"'He wasn't like that at all.'

"'He'd cast a glamour over himself,' said the old woman, 'to hide his ugliness and make himself look handsome.'

"'Then the glamour made him look as his

nature was,' said Katla. 'He was kind, loving and gentle. He walked with the girl, telling her that she was lovely, and that he loved her. And she loved him. I'm sorry. I'm not good at telling stories.'

"'No, go on,' said the old woman, her mother-in-law.

"'What is there to tell? They met often, the girl and the elf-man, and soon enough the girl was to have a child. When she went home from the sheilings her – her master demanded to know who the father was, but she said that there was no father and no child, and she wore her clothes loose, so people couldn't see her shape. And the next spring, she went to the sheilings again, eager to meet her elf-lover, who she'd met only in dreams all through the long winter. Now her master told those that went with her to watch her and never leave her alone, and so she could never see her lover – but he wanted to see her too, and he drove the animals away. The men had to go and look for them, and then the elf raised a fog, so that they spent a whole day lost.

"Under cover of the fog, the elf came to the girl, and he helped her birth her child, and wash it. And he'd brought beautiful cloths to wrap the baby in. 'I shall take our son with me until we can be together,' he said. 'There are many who will look after him kindly. But before I go,' he said, 'you must take a drink from this bottle'. And he took a bottle from his pocket and gave it to her. It was the sweetest, warmest drink that I ever –' Katla coughed and dropped the ball of wool she'd been knitting with. Stooping to pick it up, she said, '– that she ever tasted. And she was quite healed and well again, just as if she'd never had a child. When the men came back from finding the animals, they watched her closely again, but she didn't care, because she knew there would be another year, and she would see her elf-man again, and their son.'

"After saying that, Katla fell silent and didn't speak for a while.

"'What happened to the girl after that?' her mother-in-law asked.

"'Oh, there's not much more to tell. When the girl reached home her master made her marry a mortal man, against her will. And since she was made a wife, and a wife's solemn vows and promises forced on her, she determined to keep them and be a good wife. And so she was. But every beat of her heart ached for her elf-man and her child, and she never drew an easy breath or had a happy day. That is my story, the only one I know. Did you enjoy it?'

"'I'm glad to have heard it,' said her mother-in-law. 'Now I remember a girl who made a very unhappy marriage. . .' And so she started her storytelling again."

"Oh, that's very sad," said Osyth.

"Listen," said the head. "Time went on and years passed. Katla and her husband had a couple of small children, and Katla kept them clean and neat, but seemed to take little pleasure in them. This pained her husband, as he had hoped that, when they had children, she would love them, and come to love him. It didn't happen.

"Then it was haymaking time again. Katla stayed indoors, as she always did, but her husband was out in the fields, working and keeping an eye on things. And two people came across the field to him. One was tall, a man, but the other was shorter and slimmer, like a boy. It would have been hard to know them again, though, because, for all the heat, they both wore black coats with deep hoods that hid their faces.

"'Are you the master here?' said the taller of the two, the man. He had a deep voice.

" 'I am,' said the farmer.

" 'We're looking for work, my son and I,' said the stranger. 'Would you hire us for the winter?'

" 'I'll have to speak to my wife first, before I can give you an answer,' said the farmer.

" 'What?' said the man.

" 'I never hire anyone without asking my wife first, if it's all right by her. If you can wait until I get a chance to ask her—'

" 'Where is the master of the farm?' the tall man demanded.

" 'You're speaking to him,' said the farmer.

" 'I can't be. The master of a farm could make up his own mind about small things, like whether he could feed two men over the winter. He wouldn't need to ask his wife.'

" 'If you don't like the way this farm is run, you can go elsewhere,' said the farmer, but if truth was told, he thought it wearisome himself to be always asking his wife about these matters. He'd gone along with her fancy when they'd first married – but in those days he'd still thought he could win her over. Now, after all these years, when she was still as cold as ever, he was tired of trying to please her and never succeeding.

" 'It's a long road to tramp to another farm,' said the tall, hooded man. 'We'd like to stay here. We're good workers. You'll find us well worth the feeding.'

" 'Oh, all right, then,' said the farmer. He was hot and tired himself, and didn't want to tramp back to the house. 'Pitch in and help. You're hired.'

"So, at the end of that day, two more men came into the farm kitchen to be fed than had been there for breakfast. Even there they wore their hoods, but for all that, people saw Katla start when she saw them. She went round the table to her husband and said, 'Who are those two?'

" 'They'll be with us for the winter,' he said. 'They came asking for work, so I took them on.'

" 'Without asking me?' she said.

" 'You're so busy in the house, too busy to give a hand with the harvest,' he said. 'I didn't want to bother you with a little thing like that.'

" 'When we married,' she said, 'you gave your faithful promise that you would never hire men over the winter without first asking me.'

" 'Aye, well, now I've broken it,' he said.

" 'So you have,' she said. 'But my conscience is clear. Whatever comes of this will be your fault alone.' Then she went on serving the dinner and spoke not another word to her husband that night. Nor did she speak to the strangers in hoods.

"The winter wore on. The new man and his boy were, as they had said, good workers, doing everything that was asked of them willingly and doing it well. But they didn't get on so well with the other people of the farm, never having much to say to them. Most of the time they wore their hoods up and, it was an odd thing, but no matter how many times a day you met with one, and spoke with them, you would have been hard put to say what either of them looked like. They didn't sleep in the farmhouse, but made themselves a home in one of the storehouses, sleeping on top of the chests. The farmer once asked if they weren't cold out there, but the man said that they were warm enough. Katla never once asked after them, or even spoke to them, that anyone remembered. She didn't even serve them at dinner, but always sent one of the maids to their end of the table. People supposed she snubbed them because her husband had hired them without asking her permission.

"Now the New Year came, and the farm

people hung branches of green yew and holly in the house, and Katla cooked up a feast for them, and baked good pies and cakes, though she seemed no more cheerful than she ever was.

"Tell me, lassie, is it the custom in this part of the world to kiss everyone before the New Year comes in, and ask their forgiveness for any hurt you've done them in the past year?"

"Something like that," Osyth said. "At Christmas, we go to hear Communion, and we have to confess to the priest, and then kiss everyone and ask their forgiveness before we can receive it."

"Ah, this is a Christian custom," said the head. "But not so unlike the old ways, eh? Anyway, it was the time of New Year, and everyone was to make a new beginning, so they all went round. . . Katla kissed all her maids, and begged them to forgive her if she'd been sharp with them. And they kissed her, and begged her to forgive them for being clumsy or careless. Katla and her mother-in-law kissed each other and promised to try and be more patient. Katla and her husband kissed each other and promised to try and be more kind to each other – oh, and so on, all through the household. The farmer kissed his men, and they kissed him, and everybody was drinking and full of food, and all feeling very mellow and loving.

"Well, the night was nearing its end, and the New Year was going to start very soon, when the farmer said to Katla, 'What about the new hired men? Have you kissed and forgiven them?'

" 'The men you hired that you should never have hired?' she said.

" 'Now, now, Katla, we were going to be kind to each other, weren't we?'

" 'If you want to know,' she said, 'no, I haven't kissed them.'

" 'I think they have something to forgive you for,' said the farmer. 'You haven't been pleasant to them. Go and kiss them and forgive them for my fault, and let's start the New Year well.'

" 'So now, having broken your promise to me, you want me to kiss these men as well,' she said.

" 'Oh Katla, have I been such a bad husband?' said the farmer. 'For once, do something without arguing, do something to please me.'

"Katla stood. 'Very well. Where are these men?'

"It seemed they were across the yard, in the

storehouse where they'd made their lodgings. Katla wrapped her cloak around her, because it was cold outside, and she put a candle in a lantern, to guide her across the dark yard, and then she went to the door. Where she turned, looked at her husband and said, 'Goodbye.' Which people thought odd, since she was only stepping out for a few minutes.

"In the farmhouse, the people went on drinking, talking, laughing, eating. The fiddler played. The candles burned wastefully, but who cared – it was only once a year! And then folk started to think about going to bed, because they couldn't keep their eyes open. It was then they realized that Katla hadn't returned.

" 'She only went across the yard to kiss the men!' said one of the maids, and some of the farm-men sniggered, which made the farmer glower. He got a lantern of his own, and went across the yard to see what had happened to his wife. Soon, they heard him shouting, and more candles were put in more lanterns, and half the farm turned out into the cold yard.

"The hired men, and Katla, had gone. Not a sign of them was to be found in any of the out-houses or barns or byres.

"The farmer didn't say much, but he was

furious, his people could tell. 'It's too dark to search now,' he said. 'We'll look for them in the morning.' He thought his wife had run away with the hired men.

"But the next day, though they searched for miles in all directions, not a trace of any of them could be found. They asked at neighbouring farms, but no one had seen them, and no one's dogs had barked at passing strangers in the night.

" 'I'll ride to the shore,' said the farmer, 'and ask about people taking ships.'

"Then his mother spoke up and said, 'Son, I fear that if you search for the rest of your life, you'll never find Katla again in this world.'

" 'What do you mean?' he said. And then his mother told him the story Katla had told her, about the girl who had been courted by the elf-man.

" 'She was an honest girl,' said the old woman. 'When she made her wedding vows to you, she meant to keep them, though her heart wasn't in it. She made you promise never to hire men without asking her first, in case her elf-lover came looking for her. And even when he came here – with their son – and worked and ate among us, she wouldn't look at him, or smile at him. But you sent her across the yard to kiss him.'

"And it was true. Katla was never seen at any port – she boarded no ship. No farmer opened his door to her. She was never seen again."

The candles had burned lower and the heavy shadows had shifted. Osyth sighed, lay back on her bed, and was quiet for a long time. "Yes, I liked that story," she said, at last.

"I'm glad," said the head.

"The ending was sad, but happy too. It was a shame that Katla had to be so miserable for so long, but at least – do you think she was happy with her elf-man in the end?"

"If a woman can be happy among such strangers. If she can leave everything of her own world, and her children, and still be happy."

"But she was so sad as she was. It was a shame for her husband too. He loved her, but she didn't make him happy, did she?"

"It's as well to remember that love brings as much unhappiness as happiness," said the head.

Osyth turned over on the bed and looked into the head's eyes. "Is it better not to fall in love and not to marry, then?"

"Aye, and never go out in the rain either, or

get your feet wet, or be caught in the snow and get a cold nose and cold fingers. Never eat too much and get a bellyache, never drink too much and get a headache – lassie, choosing not to love would be like a fish choosing not to live in water."

"But not to marry, anyway?"

"Lassie, in this life, in this world, what will you do if you don't marry? Go into one of your nunneries?"

Osyth rolled over on to her belly, and propped her chin in her hands. "Do you know what I'm thinking? I think I'll ask my father to take me to court."

"That will be an adventure for you," said the head.

"And we shall have to take you with us, in case I become ill again. I need you, to keep me smiling, don't I? And, I'm thinking, wherever the court is, your King Penda won't be far away. Isn't that so?"

"That's so, lassie," said the head. "That is so."

THE HEAD TELLS OF PRINCES
AND GOOSE-GIRLS

"It's a pretty gel," said the old queen, King Edgar's mother. "Are you married yet?"

"No, Madam," said Osyth, with another dip. She tried not to squint. The bright sunlight from the window behind the queen was shining into her eyes.

"But you're promised?"

"No, Madam."

"What?" The queen looked up from her stitching quite crossly, but then said, "Ah, but you have no mother, do you? Still, whatever has your father been doing? We must find you a husband while you're here. I've no doubt that's why your father's brought you. He's woken up to his responsibilities, late in the day."

"Yes, Madam."

"What's that box you have there?"

"It's my head, Madam," Osyth said.

"Isn't that your head, on your shoulders?"

The queen's ladies, all sitting round her near the bower's windows, tittered.

"I mean, Madam, that in this box I have the head of Egil Grimmssen, which was given into my care."

A man's voice said, "You have the head of Egil Grimmssen?"

Startled, Osyth shaded her eyes against the bright light, and saw that there was a man sitting beside the old queen. She hadn't seen him before, because of shyness and the bright light.

"I gave that head into the keeping of my monks," said the man, and Osyth realized that this was King Edgar.

"Your head, indeed," said the queen. "If it's anyone's head, it belongs to my son. Child, how do you come to have it?"

"King, I am sorry," Osyth said. "Truly I am sorry, Madam. I was sick, and the head was brought to me and cured me. And I have kept it with me, to keep the sickness from me. Forgive me, I didn't mean to annoy anyone. I didn't think anyone would mind."

"Did you not, Miss?" said the queen. "Why have you brought it here?"

"Because Egil's lonely by himself, Madam.

He likes company. I thought you might like to hear some stories while you stitch."

A whispering passed among the queen's ladies. They looked at each other from the corners of their eyes and leaned around each other to peep at the king. It was for him to say whether the head would be seen.

"I, for one," said the old queen, "would like to see it, and hear it speak for myself."

King Edgar sighed, and then leaned forward, his elbow on his knee. "What's your name?" he asked Osyth, in a way that set the queen's ladies peeping at one another again, and smiling.

"Osyth, King."

"Osyth," the king repeated, and the ladies put their heads together again. The queen looked round at them, and said, "What's the matter now? Silly chits!"

"Open up your box, then, Osyth," said the king. "Give the old head an airing."

The box was at Osyth's feet. She knelt, opened it, lifted out the head and held it up, her hands cupped about its cheeks, for them to see. Some of the ladies turned away their faces, some peeped through their fingers. The old queen studied it calmly, and as if trying to find fault with it.

"Good day, Egil!" said King Edgar. "How have you been keeping since last we met?"

The head opened its eyes. The queen started slightly. Some of the ladies shrieked. "Oh – quiet!" she said. "Silly girls."

"You must tell me how I'm keeping," said the head. "I have no mirror."

"You look fresh as a new leaf," said the king. "How do you like it in that box?"

"I don't," said the head. "But I can hardly travel astride a horse."

"I thought I'd safely disposed of you among the monks," said the king. "But here you are again, turning up in the company of a pretty young lady." The waiting-women bent their heads over their hands to hide their smirks, and the old queen gave her son a sudden, sharp glance.

"Aye," said the head. "We've travelled a long way together, Osyth and I, and she's told me all the bits of news picked up along the road. I hear that King Penda is no better."

"A man doesn't get over a wound in a day," said King Edgar.

"A visit from me would cheer him," said the head.

"A visit from you!" said King Edgar. "I

doubt it. Have you come to make mischief, Egil?"

"I've come to tell the queen and her ladies a story," said the head.

"Then tell one," said the queen, still sharp. "Something to amuse these silly chits and stop their twittering."

"A story for silly chits," said the head. "I think I know one. Be quiet, all you silly chits, and listen! I begin."

✱ ✱ ✱

"Once there was a far-off land – don't ask me where. You could go by horse and by foot in every direction, and take ship and sail to the end of the seas, and not find this place. But it was a fair land, with fine forests and wide rivers, with high mountains and broad meadows, with cities and towns and little, hidden villages. And it had a king—"

"So I should hope," said the queen.

"And a queen," said the head. "And this king and queen had a son. His name was Prince Hart. Ah, lasses! Tall, and strong of body, and vigorous—"

The queen's ladies looked at each other and

giggled. They peeped at King Edgar, and giggled the more.

"Oh, don't encourage them," said the queen.

"A fine head of hair and a quick, gleaming eye," said the head. "A body that made him a champion at riding and wrestling. Every day he rode out to the hunt, every evening he danced, and every night he bedded—"

"Storyteller!" said the queen.

"I was going to say, Madam, that every night he bedded down in his goose-feather bed and slept the deep sleep of the young and exhausted."

"Of course you were," the queen agreed.

"Now near the royal palace, there stood a very different dwelling. A small wooden hut – dry and clean, but very poor."

"And here, no doubt, lived a penniless wood-cutter," said the queen.

"A forester, Madam, who had a large family to feed, and little to feed them with. His eldest daughter was named – she was named Osyth, and she was a lovely girl."

"A name that suited her, then," said King Edgar, smiling at Osyth, who sat on the floor, holding the head in her lap. She blushed, and smiled, but then caught the queen giving her a hard look, and lowered her face.

"She herded geese in the forest—" said the head.

Here all the ladies looked at Osyth, and tittered again at the idea of her doing such lowly work. The queen cried out, "God's Teeth! Will you cease your brainless sniggering and listen! Or, if you don't want to listen, I can find you errands to run and jobs to do elsewhere!"

All the ladies fell quiet and bowed their heads over their work.

"Young Osyth herded geese in the forest," said the head, "and often she saw Prince Hart ride out hunting. The first time she saw him, she fell in love with his bright hair and long legs; and every time she saw him after that, she loved him more."

The real Osyth peeked up at King Edgar, found him smiling at her, and hurriedly looked down.

"But she knew she could never have more of him than the sight of him as he rode by," said the head. "He never looked at her. Her heart swelled and ached with love for him, and she was sadder every day."

"Silly chit!" said the queen.

"One morning, early, before it was full light,

Prince Hart rode out on a hunt. That evening the hunt returned – but Prince Hart was not with them. In the stable yard the hunters asked, 'Is the prince home?' His horse isn't stabled, they were told. Into the palace the hunters went. 'Is the prince home?' No one had seen him. At last the head huntsman went to the king. 'It was midday,' he said, 'and the sun was bright, yet a thick fog came down round us, so we couldn't see each other. We dismounted, and went slowly and carefully, calling to each other, but none of us heard the prince calling. And when the fog lifted, and we found each other again, the prince was not among us. We hoped that he had found his way home before us – but it seems he isn't here. Is he here? Have you seen him?'

"The king hadn't seen his son. The palace was searched – not only the prince's bower, but every bower, and every outhouse. Every stable and pigsty and hen-house and dovecot. The prince was nowhere to be found.

"'A night in the forest won't do my son any harm,' said the king. "We'll find him tomorrow – if he doesn't come home himself.'

"The prince didn't come home, and parties of men went out from the palace, to search for him in all directions. He wasn't found. No news was heard of him.

"The search went on the next day, and the next. The search-parties scoured further and further from the palace, combing through forests, looking in barns, dragging ditches, crossing fells. But the prince had vanished. Nothing was seen or heard of him."

The queen had laid down her stitching and shook her head. "Terrible. Terrible."

"The king and queen mourned as if their son was dead, and the king sent out heralds, to proclaim throughout his lands that anyone who found his son and brought him home would receive half the kingdom as their reward."

"Now that I cannot think wise," said the queen, and King Edgar shook his head and laughed.

"Why?" asked the head. "Would you not give half your kingdom for your son, if he was lost?"

The queen began stitching again, and wagged her head over the problem. "Oh. . . I would. Certainly I would. But I cannot help thinking that I would live to regret it. When the wars started. But go on, storyteller, go on."

"There was another person in the kingdom who grieved for the prince's loss – who cried herself to sleep at night, and couldn't eat because she no longer saw him –"

"Osyth," said King Edgar. The queen's ladies didn't dare to giggle, but made big eyes and round mouths at each other.

"Aye, laddie. Osyth, the forester's daughter. But when she heard the king's proclamation, she was better all at once. Why sit at home and grieve, when you can go out and search? She asked her parents for a new pair of boots, which they gave her. From one of her brothers, she borrowed a warm, thick cloak. And she asked her Granny for a loaf of bread to take with her as food. 'A small loaf with my blessing, or a big loaf with my curse?' her Granny asked. What would have been your answer, lassie?"

"A small loaf with her blessing?" Osyth said.

"Good answer! A Granny's curse is a powerful thing. You never want to be cursed by your Granny. Well, with her new boots on her feet, with the borrowed cloak wrapped round her, and with the small loaf in her pack, Osyth set off.

"She walked and walked. She went by moor and stone, by stream and valley, by wood and field. I have no time to tell you how far she walked. Everyone she met had heard of the prince, but none had seen him. And then, in the middle of a bright day, as she was climbing a mountain path, a thick, grey fog came down. Nothing could she see, and only whispers and groans came to her ears. So she sat down and ate a bit of her Granny's loaf until the fog lifted."

"Because you must never wander about on a mountain-side in a fog," said Osyth, blushing at her own daring as she interrupted the story.

"Well said, lassie!" cried the head, and King Edgar said, "As wise as she is beautiful." Osyth blushed a yet deeper red, and the queen frowned.

"When the fog lifted at last," said the head, "everything looked the same, and on she went, until she saw a cave above her in the rocks. 'That might be a good place to shelter for the night,' she thought, and clambered up to have a look at it. But, when she reached it, it wasn't just a cave. Inside the cave-mouth was a wooden wall, with a wooden door in it, and the door was standing open.

"She put her head round the door and peeped inside. Torches were burning in there, lighting it with fire. The cave-walls were hung with embroidered hangings, and there were two beds, side by side. One bed was hung with curtains embroidered in gold, and the other was hung in curtains embroidered with silver.

"There was no one to be seen inside the cave, so Osyth slipped inside. As she tiptoed closer to the beds, she saw that the posts of both of them were carved with swans, holding their wings spread – silver swans and golden swans. Using one finger, she moved aside a fold of the silver curtain and keeked inside. The silver bed was empty. She went to the golden bed, and moved aside a fold of the golden curtain. When she keeked in, she saw Prince Hart asleep.

"Oh, how glad she was! She pulled back the curtains with a rattle of their rings, she called his name, she jumped on to the bed and crawled up to look at his face – but he didn't wake. She kissed his eyes, she kissed his lips, she turned back the covers and—"

"Storyteller!" said the queen.

"I was enjoying that!" King Edgar protested, while Osyth put her hands to her hot cheeks.

"You can behave, or you can go," said the queen.

"She shook him, Madam," said the head. "I was going to say, she shook him, but she couldn't wake him. Then she looked about her and, by the red light of the torches she saw that, in the head-board were scored runes, as if carved by a knife."

"Tch!" said the queen. "Who would do that to such a bed?"

"She didn't understand the runes, and thought they might be spells. Maybe that was why the prince wouldn't wake. So she saw that she would have to be clever, and brave, and bide her time. She crawled under the golden bed, and hid there."

"Not the best place to hide," said the queen. "It would be cold and draughty there, on the floor. And I know some people –" she looked about her at her young ladies – "who always look under the bed before they get in, to make sure there are no wolves or bears hiding there."

"Where would you have Osyth hide, then, Madam?" the head asked.

"I don't know. Are there no other rooms?"

"It's a cave, Madam, not a palace."

"A very well-furnished cave. Well. Is there a clothes chest, or a barrel in which she might hide?"

"The chest is full of clothes, Madam, and the barrel is full of heather-ale."

"Oh, let her hide under the bed, and get on with the story."

"Osyth lay hidden under the bed for a long time, and she did get cold, and stiff, and hungry, but she set her teeth and stayed where she was. And then she heard voices – loud voices – outside. And footsteps – thumping footsteps. Then in through the door came two ugly trows."

"Two what?" the queen asked.

"Trows, madam – elves, giantesses, boggarts, call them what you please. We have them in Orkney. An ugly sort, with noses a metre long."

"How difficult that must make life for them!"

"They have tails at the back, for balance, Madam."

"Dear me!"

"As they came into the cave, one drew in a big snifter of air through that long nose, and said, 'Fee, fi, fo, fum, I smell warm blood!' But the other cuffed her sister, and said, 'That's our darling you smell. Give over.' And this second trow-woman went up to the golden bed and said to the carved swans, 'Sing, sing, my lovely swans, and sing Prince Hart awake!'

"The carved golden swans moved their

wings, stretched their long necks, opened their beaks and sang most beautifully; and as they sang, Prince Hart woke and sat up in the golden bed. Osyth, underneath, felt the bed move as he did.

"She heard one of the trow-women say, 'Will you have something to eat, sweetheart?'

" 'I'll eat nothing that you serve,' says the prince.

" 'You'll eat when you're hungry enough,' says the second trow-woman.

"And the first one says, 'Will you marry us, darling?'

" 'No!' says the prince.

" 'Then sing, sing, my lovely swans and sing Prince Hart asleep!' And the prince fell asleep again.

"Then the two trow-women pottered about their cave. They made themselves a meal, undressed, and climbed into the silver bed. Osyth peeped out from under the bed and saw their big horny toenails, and their tails."

"And did she spend all night under the bed?" asked the queen.

"She did. The next morning she was woken by the trow-women tumbling out of their bed. 'Sing, sing, my lovely swans, and sing Prince

Hart awake!' one cried, and the golden swans sang, and the prince woke.

"'Do you want some breakfast?' one asked.

"'Not from you!' said the prince.

"'Will you marry us?'

"'Never!'

"'Then sing, sing, my lovely swans, and sing Prince Hart asleep!' He fell asleep in the blink of an eye, and soon after the trow-women left the cave.

"As soon as they were gone, Osyth crawled from under the bed – feeling cold and stiff, Madam – and limped to the door. She watched the trow-women out of sight, and then she turned to the bed and said, 'Sing, sing, my lovely swans, and sing Prince Hart awake.'

She watched the carved swans spread their wings, stretch their necks, open their beaks and sing. As they sang, Prince Hart woke, and sat up. He had never noticed her before—"

"She couldn't have been as pretty as our Osyth, then," said King Edgar, "or he would have noticed her, all right."

"Edgar," said his mother, the queen. "This girl is going to be one of my ladies, trusted to my care by her father. I'll thank you to keep your remarks to yourself."

King Edgar smiled.

The head kept silent, as interrupted story-tellers will, until the queen said, "Go on, go on!"

"Prince Hart had never noticed Osyth the goose-girl before, but now there was no one else to see. And she was a beautiful girl – even more beautiful if you've seen no one for weeks but ugly trow-women. 'Who are you?' he said.

"'I'm Osyth, the forester's daughter, and I've come to find you and take you home.'

"'Glad I am to see you,' said the prince, 'but I think neither of us will ever see home again. I'm the prisoner of two trow-women – I think we are a world away from home – and if they catch you here, they'll eat you.'

"'We'll win home if we set our minds to it,' Osyth said. 'I've had a long, cold night to think, and what you must do is this. When they come home and offer you something to eat, take it—'

"'Eat trow-food!' cries the prince. 'And become a trow!'

"'*Pretend* to eat it,' says Osyth. 'Hide it in the bed. If you're hungry, I've got a bit of bread with me.' So they sit on the golden bed and share a crust of Granny's bread. 'When they ask if you'll marry them, you must say, yes—'

" 'Marry a trow! Never!'

" 'Say you'll marry them only if they'll tell you what these runes mean, carved on the bed – and only if they'll tell you what they do all day. I shall be under the bed, listening. Once we know how they spend their time, and what these runes mean, we may be able to make a plan.'

" 'I don't know,' says the prince.

" 'You haven't done too well by yourself,' says Osyth. 'So try my way.' And he agrees.

"So they spent the rest of the day talking, and finding that they liked each other well enough. When the light started to fade, Osyth said, 'Now I'd better put you back to sleep.'

" 'Oh, don't do that,' said the prince. 'It's horrible, to feel yourself falling asleep, without being able to help yourself. I'll lie down and pretend to be asleep.'

" 'That might not work,' said Osyth. 'You know how it is with magical things. If these carved swans can sing a spell, might they not tell the trow-women that you're not asleep? No, better let the swans sing you to sleep, so they can wake you again.'

"The prince thought about it, and agreed. So Osyth told the swans to sing him asleep, and then she kept watch at the door of the cave. When she saw the two trow-women stomping back, she dived under the bed.

"In came the trow-women, their noses waggling before them and their tails dragging behind. One of them started to cook a meal, the smell of which was not good, and the other one stood beside the bed – Osyth could see her big, dirty feet – and said, 'Sing, sing, my lovely swans, and sing Prince Hart awake.'

"The swans spread their wings, stretched their necks and sang, and Prince Hart woke. 'Do you want something to eat, sweetheart?' asked the trow-woman.

"'I'm so hungry, I can no longer refuse,' said the prince. The trow-women were delighted, and wagged their tails. They rushed to serve him a bowl of whatever it was they were eating. Prince Hart pretended to eat it, but really he threw it under the bed, or stuffed it beneath the covers, or threw it into the cave's dark corners – whichever he had the chance to do without being seen."

"The state that bed will be in!" said the queen.

"'Now, darling, will you marry us?' asked the trow-women.

" 'I can't marry you when I know nothing about you', said the prince. 'When we mortals marry, we know everything about each other.'

"Ha!" said the queen.

" 'Ask whatever you want to know – we'll tell you!' said the trows.

" 'Well, what do you do with yourselves all day?"'asked the prince.

" 'We gather firewood for our fire,' said one trow.

" 'We catch fish for our dinner,' said the other.

" 'And men, sometimes.'

" 'Hush!' said her sister. 'We catch squirrels and rats and owls, for the pot.'

" 'And is that all you do – work?' asked the prince. 'Do you never entertain yourselves?'

" 'Oh, sometimes,' said one of the trows, 'just for fun, we—'

" 'Sister!' said the other.

" 'We take our life-egg—'

" 'Sister!'

" 'What's the matter? We take our life-egg and we toss it from one to the other!'

" 'Your life-egg!' said the prince. 'But eggs break so easily! What would happen if you ever dropped it?'

" 'Never you mind!' said the other trow.

" 'We'd die!' said the first. 'That's what makes it so amusing!'

" 'I feel I know you much better already,' said the prince. 'There's just one other thing I'd really like to know.'

" 'What's that?' asked the trow.

" 'These runes carved on the head of the bed here. What do they mean?'

" 'Don't tell him everything!' cried the one trow, in a pet, but the first trow said,

" 'Oh, that's a spell. It means: *Glide, slide, my good bed, wherever I want to go.*'

As soon as she spoke, the bed began to move, gliding towards the door of the cave.

" 'Oh, stop, stop!' said the trow. '*Stop, stop, my good bed: halt here.*' And the bed stopped. 'Now will you marry us?'

" 'Certainly – tomorrow or the day after,' said the prince. 'But now I'm tired after that big meal and I'd like to sleep.'

The trows sighed. 'All right,' they said, and told the swans to sing him to sleep."

"I hope," said the queen, "that the girl hiding under the bed is taking note of how smoothly her prince lies. It may stand her in good stead in the future."

"Cynical old besom," said the head.

"Thank you," said the queen. "Call me 'old and wise', and you've said the same thing."

"The next morning the trows woke the prince by setting the swans to sing, and they offered him breakfast. He pretended there was nothing he'd like better, but hid the bone-bread and the lumps of half-cooked meat under the bed and under the pillows.

" 'Come out to the woods with us,' said one of the trows. 'Help us catch squirrels.'

" 'Thank you,' said the prince, 'but it looks as if it's going to rain to me. And after that big breakfast, I'd rather have a nap.'

So the trows called on the swans to sing him to sleep again, and went off to hunt.

When she was sure the trows were far away, Osyth came from under the bed, and told the swans to sing Prince Hart awake. 'Am I awake now, or asleep?' he asked. 'I'm not dreaming you, am I?'

" 'I'm real enough,' Osyth said, and climbed on the bed beside him. She said, '*Glide, slide, my good bed, to where the trow sisters are.*' The bed started to move. It tilted, and lifted, and floated a hand's span above the ground. They clung to the bedposts. Out of the cave glided the bed, down the hillside, and into the wood. '*Glide,* slide, my good bed,' said Osyth, 'to where the trow sisters play their egg game.' The bed made a sharp turn, went round some beech trees, hid for a while behind a briar thicket, and then rose high and steep to hover above a tall oak tree.

"Osyth and Prince Hart heard wild laughter, and looked down into a glade. There were the trow sisters, roaring and tossing something small and bright between them. Sometimes they had to jump up high to catch it, and sometimes they had to throw themselves low, and that was when they laughed most loudly.

"Osyth watched carefully and then, just as the egg hung in the air between the sisters, she screamed a high, sudden and piercing scream. The sister who was to catch the egg gave a yell herself, and started and looked round – and missed.

" 'No!' yelled the other trow, just as the egg hit the ground and smashed.

"Both trow sisters fell dead.

" 'That's the end of them,' said Osyth. 'Glide, slide, my good bed, and take us back to the cave.'

"Back to the cave went the bed. They searched the cave and found much of value – brooches, swords, belt-buckles, coin, all scattered among old bones. They loaded it on to the bed, climbed aboard themselves, and Osyth said, '*Glide, slide, my good bed, home to my parents.*' On the way, Osyth told the prince how his father had promised half the kingdom to anyone who could find him and bring him home. 'And I've found you, and I've brought you home, so half your kingdom belongs to me now.'

" 'It would anyway,' said the prince, 'because I am going to wed you.'

"The bed floated through a dense fog, and then settled outside Osyth's little cottage in bright sunshine. 'Hurry up to the palace,' Osyth said, 'and tell your father about the wedding. I'll wait here until you send for me.'

"Oh, ho, ho," said the old queen.

"So off to the palace went Prince Hart. Everyone was amazed to see him come strolling in. Skivvies and pot-wallopers came pouring out of the kitchens. Stable lads and muck-shifters came hurrying round from the stables. Ladies and gentlemen pushed and shoved and leaned out of windows to gawp. And the king and queen came running. They were overjoyed, and called for drink, and a feast, and it was a whole day before Prince Hart could get them to listen to anything he said.

"But when they were quieter, he said to

them, 'I hear that you promised to give half your kingdom to whoever found me and brought me home.'

" 'But you came home by yourself, dear boy!' cried the king. 'So we've no need to worry about that!'

" 'I've been trying to tell you,' said Prince Hart, 'that I was found and rescued by Osyth the forester's daughter. I would never have reached home if it hadn't been for her. And I want to marry her.'

" 'What?' said the king.

" 'A forester's daughter?' said the queen. 'Don't be a silly boy!' "

"Quite right," said the old queen. "Exactly what I should say myself."

" 'Your wedding is all arranged,' said the king. 'It has been since you were two. There's no question of your wedding a forester's daughter.'

" 'Isn't it better that I marry Osyth?' asked Prince Hart. 'After all, that will keep the kingdom together.'

" 'Keep the kingdom to – Oh! You don't really think I was going to give half the kingdom to a forester's daughter, do you?' said the king. 'Have some sense, lad! We'll give her some shiny trinkets, that'll make her happy.'

" 'Give her a little dowry,' said the queen. 'Enough to attract a comfortable farmer. That would be more than generous.' "

"I quite agree," said the old queen.

" 'Enough of this!' said Prince Hart. 'I shall marry Osyth, and there's an end of it!'

" 'We shall see about that!' said his father, and he had Prince Hart locked up. Immediately he ordered a great wedding feast prepared, and sent men on fast horses to fetch the princess he had always intended his son to marry.

"Osyth was waiting at her father's cottage for the prince to send her word. She heard nothing from him, but she saw the comings and goings into and out of the palace as cart-loads of food and drink were taken in, and guests arrived. Word soon spread through the countryside that Prince Hart was marrying a foreign princess."

"No," said King Edgar, shaking his head. "She can't have been such a charmer as our Osyth." He smiled at his mother, who had turned her gaze on him.

"Goose-girl Osyth knew what to do. She climbed on to her bed and said, *Glide, slide, my good bed, to where Prince Hart is marrying the foreigner.* And the bed tilted, and lifted, and hovered, and flew away, over the castle walls, and in at a door, and bumped down on the tiled floor of the hall where Prince Hart and the foreign princess were just about to join hands.

"Osyth stood up on the bed, put her hands on her hips, and said, 'Is this the one who travelled hard and far and passed through the mist to find you? Who woke you from the trows' spell? Who showed you how to break the egg? Who you promised to marry?'

"Now Prince Hart had been bullied and nagged by his parents into doing his duty – but when he saw Osyth, he said, 'No – you are the one!' And he dropped the hand of the foreign princess and jumped on to the bed. 'Fly us away from them all!' he said.

"'Oh no,' she said. 'Half this kingdom is mine.' And she said, '*Sing, sing, my lovely swans, and sing all these strangers asleep!*'

"The golden swans spread their wings, stretched their necks, opened their beaks and sang – and everyone except Osyth and Prince Hart fell asleep. They fell into a long, long, deep sleep and couldn't be awakened.

"Osyth and Prince Hart had them stacked in store-rooms, out of the way, and left them to sleep. They married, and ruled the kingdom together, and ruled it very well. And that's the end. Did you like it, Madam?"

"Well enough," said the queen. "What's the moral?"

"Why, that a prince – or even a king – can make a very good marriage to a girl who isn't a princess."

"If she's well-born and has a little wealth to sweeten matters," said the queen. "Osyth. Osyth – you, gel! Did you think I was speaking to the forester's daughter? Would you like to be one of my ladies?"

"Oh!" said Osyth. "Well. I."

"Yes or no, gel. Am I worthy to be favoured by your attentions or not?"

Osyth blushed. "Oh, of course, Madam. Yes, Madam! Yes, please, Madam, let me be one of your ladies."

"You had better fetch your things and have them brought to my lodgings," said the Queen. "Leave Master Head here with us. For safe-keeping." Her eyes shifted from her stitching to Osyth with one fierce, darting look. "Go, then!"

Osyth shoved the head, rather roughly, back into its box, and ran.

7

THE HEAD TELLS A TALE
AT A FEAST

King Edgar's feast-hall was long and high, lit by firelight and candles. The walls were hung with hangings whose embroidered huntsmen or striding warriors stirred at the edge of sight in the fading, rising, flickering light. High above, in the rafters, were darkness and shadows: up there the skeins of grey wood-smoke drifted and broke in the breeze from the high, unglazed windows.

Below, the heat of the long-fires and the crowded people was fierce, and faces were red with drink and wet with sweat. A continual buzz of chatter and laughter crashed into loud huzzas and bellowed toasts. Bright colours of tunics and headbands – scarlet, green, blue – blazed out in full light, and muted into brown and grey in the shadows. Gold gleamed, in brooches, buckles and rings. Garnets lit to red fire, and died to dull purple: brilliant enamels shone.

Thane Redwald, Osyth's father, sat at King

Edgar's own table, an honour he had never expected. Behind him, on the bench where the women sat, was Osyth, with the king's mother, and his unmarried sisters. She clasped her hands together tightly, and gazed with delight over the bright colours and glitter of the feast.

High above a small brown sparrow was buffeted by the wind through a window, and found itself in heat and clamour, flying through the smoke, din and bright golden fire-light of the king's hall. Bewildered, it circled above the feast, its cheeping unheard, and then, by chance, found another window and flew through it, into cold winds and darkness again. On it flew, seeking a roost, leaving the king's hall far behind.

Within the hall music played, and dancers danced, and tumblers performed, turning somersaults over the fires and springing on to one another's shoulders until those uppermost were lost in the smoke. But when the people were full-fed, and their bellies were heavy, then they called for some quieter, more thoughtful entertainment – a song or a story.

The king, seated in his high-backed, carved and gilded chair at the high table, gave an order; and a servant went running and came back carrying a large, square box, which he gave into the king's hands. The king set the box at the front of the high table, where everyone could see it. He lifted the box's lid, let down the front – and there, displayed in the box, was the head.

"Now," said King Edgar, "we shall hear a story from the storyteller of our prisoner, King Penda. We shall hear a story from the famous Egil Grimmssen."

So deep a silence fell on the hall that the logs in the long-fires could be heard spitting and crackling as bubbles of sap burst; the ash could be heard falling, and sleepy birds chittering in the rafters above. Everyone there had heard of the miraculous head, but few had seen it. Many stood, the better to see this strange thing. A deep groan of astonishment and horror seemed to rise from the floor when the head opened its eyes and looked at them all.

"A feast-hall," said the head. "Where is my king? Is he here?"

"No," said King Edgar. "He is not."

"Then when will the storyteller be given his reward?" asked the head. "All I wish is to be given to my king. Why is your brother-king not invited to your feast, Edgar? Are you still afraid of him?"

All those people gathered together there in the hall drew in a long breath – it seemed that the fires and candle-flames fluttered in it.

"King Penda is not here," said Edgar, "because he is sick."

"Then take me to him!" said the head.

"There is no need for alarm," said King Edgar. "He has the best of lodgings, and the best of care. He will be well again."

"When will I be taken to him?"

"Not before you have honoured my feast with a story," said King Edgar, and he glanced aside at Osyth where she sat on the women's bench, her face flushed with the heat, her eyes wide and shining, her mouth smiling.

"Let all gathered here tonight be witnesses!" cried the head. "The payment I ask for my story is that I be given to my king! Will you pay me that, Edgar?"

"Let all here be the witnesses," said Edgar, "that if I don't pay you that, I shall pay you nothing."

"If such word-chopping and trickery is all I'm offered," said the head, "then I shall offer little in return. What do you want to hear?

Some fine tale of battles and slaughter? Of thanes and kings, of loyalty and betrayal? Of dragons and night-comers challenged and overcome? No. I shall tell you a little, little tale – of Willehad, the servant man."

The king seated himself, and everyone in the hall sat too, in silence, ready to listen to whatever tale the head chose to tell.

✠ ✠ ✠

"Once, long ago," said the head, "in a land where cockle-shells were silver bells, there lived a king who kept a great and numerous household. And to that great royal household there came, one winter's night – leaving a trail of black footsteps across a white, frozen land – a boy, who begged at the kitchens for food and shelter from the cold, and work, so that he might go on eating. His name was Willehad. He was taken in, given a bowl of pease-porridge to eat and a place by the fire to sleep, in the ashes. The next day he was set to fetching and carrying, and chopping and scouring and scrubbing.

"He was a slender, pretty lad, but stronger than he looked, and did more than he was asked, and did it well and willingly. He learned too, all that he was shown, and soon he was no longer a mere greasy kitchen-hand, but an officer of the kitchen, approving or discarding the produce brought in from the farms. And so well did he do that job, that soon he was an officer of the table, seeing to the laying of clean clothes and the setting out of dishes and salt and horns. He made sure that there was always a harpist or a juggler at hand, if the king wanted entertainment, and that the tables were cleared swiftly and quietly.

"'All is order,' said the king, 'since Willehad came to me. He is the very flower of serving men.' So well pleased was the king with Willehad's service that he made the young man the overseer of his whole house – the kitchens, the tables, the bedchambers, the court, the breweries, the dairies, the stables, the kennels, the mews – Willehad saw to the ordering of them all. And well were they ordered.

"But there are quick, sharp eyes at a court. When the king smiled at Willehad, it was seen and noted. When the king watched Willehad leaving a room, when he asked after him, it was all seen and remembered. 'The king has a favourite,' it was said. When the king and

Willehad played together at chess, it was said, 'Are there no thanes who can play chess, that the king must play with a serving man?'

"And soon stories were brought to the king about his favourite. They wished to help Willehad – that is why they told these tales, only out of love and concern for him. Something troubled the king's flower of serving men, troubled him so deeply that it disturbed his sleep. Every night those who slept in chambers near him heard him cry out. If the king would only stay wakeful one night, he would hear for himself.

"The king knew that these tale-bearers were jealous of Willehad, but, sure enough, he saw that his favourite was looking pale and tired. When asked if he was ill, or if anything was wrong, he answered, 'I am well, and nothing is wrong, nothing.'

"So the king went one night to a chamber next to the one where Willehad slept, and he waited. In the quiet deeps of the night, when all were asleep, the king slipped into Willehad's chamber, and he waited there. Willehad slept and, for all the king's determination to keep watch, he nodded himself – and was shocked awake by a cry of, 'Thieves! Thieves!'

He started to his feet and looked all round – but there was no one in the chamber except Willehad. Still asleep, he was turning in his bed, and now he cried, 'Blood, oh, blood! Oh God! Oh, my mother!'

"While the king stood at the foot of the bed, appalled, Willehad fell quiet again, and slept, and made no more outcry. Puzzled, and distressed, the king crept away.

"The next day he sent for Willehad and asked him, 'My flower of serving men – why do you dream of thieves and blood? What troubles you?'

"Willehad started a little and coloured, so the king was sure that he knew what was meant by 'thieves and blood'. But he said, 'I have no such dreams, King.'

" 'You are overheard,' said the king. 'Every night you cry out and are troubled in your sleep. Won't you tell me, as a friend, so I can help, what troubles you?'

"Willehad said, 'You are kind, and I thank you for your good wishes, but nothing troubles me. A man will have bad dreams from time to time. I beg you, don't trouble yourself on my account.'

" 'What if, my flower of men,' said the king,

'what if I order you, as your king, to tell me what troubles you?'

" 'I dream of thieves and blood,' Willehad said. 'When I wake, I forget it. Now you know all. What are your orders for today, King?'

" 'I see,' said the king, 'that you mean to keep your own mind. Tomorrow morning, early, I mean to go hunting.'

"Willehad bowed his head. 'All will be ready.'

"The king and his hunting party left at first light the next morning, and rode out to the forest. They rode west, they rode north, with pounding of hoofs and blowing of horns. It was noon when the king thought it very silent, and looked about him, and saw no one. The wide forest rides were empty of all but trees.

" 'This is strange,' said the king to himself. 'But if the Gods have sent me adventure, then I will meet it!' And he rode on, looking about him for what might happen.

"From a thicket there started a lovely stag, white as milk. Never had the king seen his like. He kicked his horse to a gallop and gave chase.

"The stag leaped, he bounded, as if he would leave the earth and fly. He vanished into thickets, trampling through the brambles – he would be lost, and then his white hide gleamed in the green shadow of oaks. The king lost him and, with sweat coating his face, despaired – but heard the stag bellowing from behind. Turning his horse, he saw the shining white antlers and saw again the fleeing deer – and spurred his horse after it, ducking to save himself from branches and thorns.

" 'Such a stag as this cannot belong to this world!' the king cried to his horse, to his hounds. 'It can only do me harm. But I'll not turn back now!'

"All day he rode in exhausting chase, until his horse was trembling and wet with sweat, until the king was jarred and scratched, and his hair torn and tangled with leaves. Never did he lose the white stag, for it always called to him, or flew across his path, so he knew it was an enchanted animal he followed, and he was full of wonder. The chase did not end until evening, when the sun darted low through the trees and dazzled his eyes. Then, in a forest clearing, the stag halted and stood, its head up, staring at the king. Seeing that the stag no longer ran from him, the king reined in his horse and jumped down, drawing his sword.

"The stag was not there. It vanished, and the darkness drew closer.

" 'I am haunted!' the king said. 'But I must rest!' And he threw himself down in the soft grass of the clearing.

"For a time he was too tired to look about him, but then he gathered himself up and, since that he would have to spend the night in the forest, did what he could for his horse, unsaddling it and rubbing it down with grass. As he did so, he looked about, and saw that the glade held the ruins of a house.

"When his horse was grazing, he went to look at the ruin, and thought that it had been a big, comfortable house, though not grand. It had been burned. The stones and timbers were charred, the fallen thatch blackened and burned to ash.

"Close to the burned house there was a long, grassy mound, very like a grave, and the king stood beside it. He thought he had never known a lonelier, nor a more silent place. The sun, sinking, glared red through the black trees and, just as darkness fell, a whiteness came fluttering and lighted on the burned stone of the house. It stretched up its neck and sang – a soft, sweet sound in the darkness. But the king was amazed to hear words come from a dove's throat. For the dove sang:

> '*I weep for the day my love became*
> *The famous flower of serving men.*'

"The king was the more shocked to hear the bird use his name for his favourite, Willehad. He cried out, 'I know there is magic here. Come bird, if speak you can, speak plain – what of the famous flower of serving men?'

"Evening mist entered the glade, coiling between the trees, twisting itself into shapes. As, bewildered, he watched the ghosts, the king heard the voice of the dove.

> '*Twas her mother did her deadly spite,*
> *Sending thieves in dark of night,*
> *Put our servants all to flight,*
> *Burned our bower, slew her knight.*'

"Through the grey mist and the forest's darkness, the house seemed to burn again, and dark figures struggled, screamed and fled about it. The king watched, shivering, now running forward to help, now falling back, for though the sights and sounds were so real they made him shudder, yet he knew it was all a vision.

> 'They feared to do her any harm,
> But they slew the baby in her arms,
> And left her naught to wrap him in,
> But the bloody sheet that he lay in.

> 'They left her naught to dig their grave
> But the bloody sword that slew her babe,
> And all alone our grave she made,
> And all alone sore tears she shed.'

"In the darkness, the king glimpsed the form of a woman, kneeling and toiling to scrape and dig a grave; and he could hear her sobs, but couldn't help her.

> 'Oh, think you not her heart was sore,
> When she threw the dirt on their yellow hair,
> And think you not her heart was woe
> When she turned her round away to go?

> 'She cut her locks and changed her name
> From Fair Eleanor to Sweet Willehad,
> And went to court to serve her king,
> As the famous flower of serving men.

'And I weep, I weep and make my moan,
From dawn of day to fall of sun,
I weep for the day my love became
The famous flower of serving men.'

"With the last note of its song, the dove vanished. The king stood alone in the forest clearing, in the dark, between the grave and the ruined house. Still, it seemed to him, he could hear the sounds of flames, and of screams and cries – but coming as if from a great distance.

"While he was still astonished, the darkness was seeped through with light, growing paler and paler. The shapes of the trees stood, dark, against a sky washed with pink as the sun rose. Colour came slowly: the green of the grass, the red of leaves touched with cold. And now the king looked about at the ruined house and the grave, and it no longer seemed a strange, ghostly place. He remembered the house from years before, when it had not been burned and ruined – and there had been no grave.

"The king went to his horse and saddled it, took its reins and led it on the long, weary way home. With every step, one thought came to his mind, one image – his head was filled by the famous flower of serving men.

"And with every step his anger grew fiercer, to think that such a crime had been committed in his land, and he had known nothing of it.

"When he came close to his palace, he mounted his horse again, and presently rode in through his gates, with cheers from his guards. He rode on into the yard before his great hall, and it was crowded with brightly-dressed lords and ladies who, hearing the news that the king had returned from his night lost in the forest, came out to welcome him. And there, standing before all of them, and bowing, was his famous flower of serving men, dressed all in black.

"The king rode towards him and, as Willehad looked up in surprise, the king leaned down from his saddle, took his servant man under the arms and lifted him up to sit before him on his horse. A gasp of surprise went up from the lords and ladies at that – but a silence fell when the king, before them all, kissed his serving man on the lips.

"Then the king looked round and laughed at the shocked and staring faces. He shouted out, so all could hear, 'Bow, bow all of you – bow to your queen-to-be, Fair Eleanor!'

"Then he dismounted and lifted Eleanor

down. Grooms led his horse away. Taking Eleanor by the hand, he led her into the hall. Every courtier, and every servant who could escape work, followed, agog to know more.

"The king took his seat in the hall, and pulled Eleanor to sit on the chair beside him. 'You would not tell me of your dream,' he said, 'but now I will tell you of it. *Thieves!* you cried, *Thieves! Blood! Blood!* Those were the thieves who came in the night, sent by your mother – the thieves who burned your house and killed your man and babe.'

"She gaped at him. 'How do you know?'

"'I have been to the place: I have seen the burned house and the grave. A white stag led me there, and a white bird told me the tale.'

"Eleanor bowed her head into her hands and wept. The king knelt beside her chair, took her in his arms and comforted her. 'Tell me only this,' he said. 'Were these murderers truly sent by your mother?' Eleanor sobbed, and nodded, and nodded. 'Then I shall ride another hunt for this she-wolf and her pack.'

"The king called up women and gave his famous flower of serving men into their hands, telling them to care for her well, and find her a queen's clothes. He would take no rest himself, but set out at once, with guards and captains. They found Eleanor's mother at home and arrested her, together with the men who had carried out her orders, and they brought them back to the palace as prisoners.

"After the king had slept and eaten, the woman was brought before him and before Eleanor, who now sat beside the king in the clothes of a queen. Eleanor, it was seen, could not look at her mother, and gripped the arms of her chair until her fingers were white.

" 'You are charged,' said the king, 'with sending men to burn down your daughter's home, to murder her man and murder her babe. What do you say?'

" 'I sent those men,' said the woman. 'I gave them those orders. It was my right.'

" 'Your right?' said the king. 'These are strange words to me.'

" 'I had planned to marry my daughter to a man with land and riches, but she defied and dishonoured me by running away to live with a nothing, a nobody, in a squalid hut in the forest. It was my right to punish her.'

" 'Even if that were so, you had no right to murder a man.'

" 'I told you, he was a nothing – and he

had spoiled my goods. He deserved it.'

"'And your grandchild?'

"'It was no grandchild of mine, and it should never have been born.'

"'Woman,' said the king, 'you are condemned by your own words. A bonefire shall be built, here, in the yard. You shall be set on top of it, and you shall burn.'

"Then Eleanor slipped from her chair and knelt at the king's side. 'Let her live!'

"'She is a murderer!'

"'She is my mother!'

"The king bent over her and said, 'I must keep the law in this, my land. How can I execute the men who stabbed to death your man and babe, yet set free her who ordered them to do it? Or am I to set them all free? Is it to be said that I smile on murder?'

"Eleanor laid her head on his knees and said only, 'She is my mother!'

"The proud woman standing before the king said, 'That whore is not my daughter and I am no mother of hers!'

"The king looked up and said, 'You have an unlucky mouth. If you are not her mother, then what do I care? Take her away and burn her!'

"A tall bonefire was made in the yard, of bundles of thorn, and the woman, Eleanor's mother, was tied on top of it, and it was lit. The thorns bloomed with flames, red and yellow, and crackled and smoked – and as the flames rose around the woman, and caught on her clothes, on her hair, on her cheek, her servants, the murderers, were hanged nearby.

"Eleanor, that flower of serving men, was married to the king, and had other babies – and the body of the first was brought from its lonely grave in the forest and buried in the royal graveyard.

"And that is my tale! I give it to you – take it, change it, and let it make its way back to my ear by another's tongue."

✠ ✠ ✠

There was applause and cheers, and pounding on tables and throwing of bread in the air. Osyth, on the women's bench behind the king's table, clapped furiously and laughed, proud of her friend, the head.

"A poor tale, I thought it," said the queen, the king's mother. "Women are always to blame, it seems to me, and doubly to blame if they are mothers. What is wrong, I'd like to know, in wishing your children to make good marriages?"

"But Mother," said one of her daughters, "she didn't love the man her mother wanted her to marry!"

"Silly chit! A lot of nonsense is talked about love. There is far more to be considered in a good marriage than love!"

King Edgar was holding up his arms, throwing shadows over the walls and table. Gradually the noise in the hall died, until the king could be heard. "It is happy," he said, "that the tale was of a marriage. For I mean to marry!"

The din rose again, with cheers, stampings, clapping.

The king had turned from the hall to the woman's bench. And he was holding out his hand to Osyth. She looked aside and saw horror on the queen's face and on her own father's. But when she looked at the king, he was still holding out his hand to her. So she took it and was pulled to her feet and brought forward to the table, to look out over the crowded hall, the red, beery faces, the bright colours, the sparkling gold.

"This," shouted the king, "this is your queen!"

And if the noise had been loud before, now it rolled and roared and seemed fit to crack the wooden hall open like a nut. While the noise crashed on, Osyth put her mouth close to the king's ear and shouted, "I know what I want for my wedding gift!"

He looked at her, grinning. "What?"

She leaned her mouth close to his ear again. "I want you to give the head back to his King Penda." When Edgar looked at her again, his eyes widening and his mouth opening, she shouted, "That is all I want and all I will accept!"

King Edgar bowed his head and nodded.

8

THE HEAD KEEPS ITS PROMISE

And so the head of Egil Grimmssen, the storyteller, was brought to the king he had served, Penda.

He was carried, in his box, into a chamber that was lit only by one candle and a dying fire.

There was little furnishing except a stool and, built against the wall, a closet bed. Its carved doors were closed.

One of the men escorting the head pulled open a door of the closet. Inside, it was full of darkness.

A hand seized a tangle of the head's hair, lifted it from its box and thrust it into the closet. "There!" said a voice. "There is your king! Enjoy each other's company!"

Then there was laughter, and the clapping closed of a box, and footsteps going away.

The head was left lying on the pillow of a bed, beside another head. "Penda!" said the head. "King!" There was no answer, not even the merest scraping of breath. Neither was there any movement. Then the head knew that King Penda, who had been sick, was dead.

"I shall keep my promise," said the head. "At least I shan't be interrupted!

"It's a tale of a king who came to his crown young. Barely out of boyhood, he was. He had to be lifted on to the throne, and then his feet dangled and didn't touch the floor.

"'How can I rule?' he said. 'I'm too young, I know nothing.'

"'You are the king,' said the people around him. 'You must rule.'

"'I need help,' he said. 'Bring me the wisest men of the kingdom.'

"Who are the wisest men? How do you know them? Can their wisdom be measured by the metre or by the cup? Nevertheless men were found, who were considered wise, and they came before the young king.

"'I need help,' he said. 'Before I take my decisions, I need to know what has happened in the world before me, what people have done, and how their decisions worked out. I want you wise men to make for me a history of the world. I want you to write in it of the doings of all the men that ever were, for my guidance.'

"The wise men looked at each other, and muttered. One spoke up and said, 'King, this will take many, many years.'

"'Be as quick as you can,' said the king. 'I must have the book.'

"Away went the wise men, to a quiet spot, and started work. They sent messengers into every part of the world, asking for knowledge. They bought and gathered together every book of history and manners and philosophy, and they burned many candles as they sat up late of nights, reading them. They wrote, and they argued and they questioned, and they wrote, and they thought; and the papers mounted up, day by day, week by week, month by month, year by year. Some of the wise men gave up in despair and went away to be ditch-diggers, some died and were replaced by others, some toiled on and grew old. But they finished their history of all the people of the world, and their decisions, and what came of them. It took them thirty years and I think it was a rushed job.

"But it was finished. The precious manuscripts were loaded on to the backs of a team of pack-ponies, and the wise men loaded themselves into carts, and away they all went, ponies and horses, books and carts and wise-men and drovers, off to the palace of the king.

"When they reached the palace and demanded admission, no one knew who they were, or knew anything about a history of the world demanded by the king. The wise-men, and their baggage, and their pack-ponies and drovers, all had to wait outside the palace gates while questions were asked inside. At last a richly dressed servant came out and apologized for keeping them waiting. The king himself remembered them, and they were to be admitted at once and given the best lodgings. The king would see them as soon as he had finished holding court.

"'So he's holding court, eh?' said one of the wise men. 'He didn't wait for our book before making his decisions, then.'

"When the wise men came before the king at last, they saw – and some of them were surprised – that he was no longer the little boy whose feet had dangled as he'd sat on the throne. He was now a large man, at the end of his youth. 'You have my book?' he said.

"'King, we have.'

"'We have made an overview of every king whose deeds and laws we could discover since the world began, of every great landowner and merchant, of every scholar and churchman, every writer and artist and music-maker, of every queen and every woman of influence.'

" 'Such a work of scholarship has never been known!'

" 'I'm glad to hear it!' said the king. 'Every day I've felt the need of it. I couldn't wait for it – you know, every day there are decisions to be made. Shall this town be allowed a market? Shall this one be allowed to build a bridge? Should this tax be revoked or should it be increased? Who shall be allowed to marry this heiress? Did this man move his neighbour's land-markers? Should more ships be built – should this town be fortified? I tell you, it's endless, and someone has to decide – and that someone is me. Bring me my book! I know I shall learn from it.'

"So the wise men began bringing in the book. It wasn't a book. It was heaps and heaps of manuscript, all written over in tiny hand-writing. Pony after pony was unloaded and pile after pile of paper was mounded up. The king watched with ever-growing astonishment.

" 'Stop! Stop!' he cried. 'I cannot read all this!'

" 'King, there are ten more ponies to be

unloaded, and we haven't yet started on the carts.'

" 'It's too much! Every day I hold court, listen to pleas and petitions and depositions. I read when I can, but I have no time to read all this!'

" 'But King, you asked for a history of the world.'

" 'I was a small boy,' said the king. 'I had no idea how old the world was, or how many people have lived in it, or how much they have done. And since then, I've had so little time to think. No, what you must do is take all this away and make me a summary.'

" 'A summary, King!' cried all the wise men, aghast. They looked around them at the towers of manuscripts.

" 'Yes, a summary. After all, you've done all the hardest work. Now skin it, and gut it and bone it, and bring me only the choicest flesh of it. The people who made the most difference, their best decisions and their outcomes. That's what I need to know.'

"Sighing and disappointed, the wise men gathered up their manuscripts and loaded them on the pack-ponies again, and returned to their quiet spot and their studies. Some, worn out, left, but other, fresher men came to help in the work.

"The wise men read through the thousands of pages they'd written. They discussed and argued about which people had been the wisest – and when they'd decided on them, they discussed and argued which of their decisions had been the most important and which could be ignored.

"They burned candles again, working late into the night, rewriting what they had written. They shortened it so much that, at the end, they could load the manuscripts on only five ponies. It had taken them fifteen years.

"This time they had sent word ahead of who they were and why they were coming, and they were welcomed at the palace gate and taken before the king immediately.

"The king was an old man, with white hair and a white beard. When the manuscripts were piled before him, he said, 'You've done well – a great work. But I must ask you to do more. I have no time to read even this. I grow old. I cannot work as long as I used, yet there is still the same work to be done. I have less time than ever to read. I must ask you, good men, to take away this, your great work, and cut it down to one short book – a slim book that I might have time to read.'

" 'But King, it will no longer be what you asked for – it will no longer be a history of the world.'

" 'It must be a history of the world, but in little. Tell me who the most important were, and in what their wisdom lay. Tell me all I need to know, as a king. Tell it me in one small book.'

"So the pack-ponies were loaded again, and the wise men left. They went back to their quiet place, and they argued and discussed again, and thought deeply, and rewrote and thought again, and wrote again – and in a mere ten years they had made one small book – so small it could be carried by one man – that contained all the wisdom of the world.

"Eagerly they travelled back to the palace – where everything was quiet. 'The king is dying,' said the guards on the gate.

" 'Come quickly,' said the servant who met them inside. 'The king is on his deathbed. He is asking for you.'

"The wise men were hurried through corridors to the king's bedchamber. There he lay, raised up on pillows to help him breathe, but still drawing his breath in harsh gasps. The wise men laid their single book on the covers of the bed, where he could reach it.

" 'Good men,' he said. 'You have done great work. But I fear I shall have no time to read even this small book. All my life I have guessed at what was best to do, and fudged and muddled. If only –' Weakly he patted the cover of the book. 'If only I had had the wisdom of the world to guide me, how much better I should have done!'

" 'You have not done so badly, King,' said his steward.

" 'Fudge and muddle,' said the king. 'Even now – even now I wish I could know just a little – a taste – of that wisdom. Can you tell me? Can you tell me, in a breath, what is the wisdom of the world?'

"Everyone gathered in that bedchamber – princes and princesses, stewards and nuns and monks and wise-men, all looked at each other. Their mouths opened – and closed again. All wished to help their king, but none knew what to say.

"Then a voice spoke up in the darkness and candlelight and smoke: a small voice that said, 'I know all that anyone needs to know.'

"Everyone in the room – the wise men, the counsellors, the king's family – turned to see who had spoken. People had to shuffle aside and make way before the speaker could be seen. It was a young girl, holding a water jug. One of the lower servants, one who had been sent to creep in and out unnoticed with fresh water, in case the king wanted to drink. And she had spoken!

"Before anyone could order her away, the king said, 'What? What is the All that anyone needs to know?'

"The girl looked shyly about at all the tall men glowering at her, and it seemed she had suddenly forgotten how to speak. But the king said, 'What? What?'

"She said, 'My Granny told me. She said it all boils down to this: We are born, we suffer, and we die. There is no more to know.'

"The king heard: and then he drew his last breath and died.

"There you have it, Penda, my King. The History of the World. The Wisdom of the World. What I should have told you on the battlefield, before I lost my body and you your kingdom. We are born, we suffer, and we die. There is no more to tell."

And Egil Grimmssen's head closed its eyes for ever.